For Milo
I'll see you when the light comes back.

Guilt is not a response to anger; it is a response to one's own actions or lack of action. If it leads to change then it can be useful, since it is then no longer guilt but the beginning of knowledge. Yet all too often, guilt is just another name for impotence, for defensiveness destructive of communication; it becomes a device to protect ignorance and the continuation of things the way they are, the ultimate protection for changelessness.

    —Audre Lorde

1

---

*T*he third time's the charm. That's how the saying goes, right? I wish I felt charmed—even like the TV show kind. But now, this gift feels like a curse, a weight. My very own albatross around my neck.

But I can bear the heft of a bird, even a big one. At least my neck isn't holding my own weight in a noose. I really don't have a thing to complain about. And yet, I'm tired. Weary even. Sarah would say, "The journey is long and rocky, but at least you're moving."

IT WAS A TUESDAY IN APRIL. I had just gotten home from school, just grabbed a bowl of cheese doodles—the puffy kind, not that awful crunchy kind, and just folded my legs under me to watch *The Voice* on the DVR. I love the blind auditions: the way the contestants get so excited, and their families cry, and the judges banter. Blake and Adam had just started to go at it. . . .

But then I was standing between two high stone walls, my jeans soaked to the knee in water. A big twist of honeysuckle climbed the wall to my left, its fragrance overwhelming in this closed-off space, and just over the wall to my right, I could hear water. Big water. Moving water.

I thanked heaven that the temperature had dropped last week so the snakes were probably not in the brush around me, because I was, yet again, barefoot. (You'd think I'd have learned to just wear shoes 24-7 after the first two times this happened.) I took a few steps and climbed up out of the water onto a ledge. Now, I could hear the traffic to my left, and I recognized Highway 60. I knew exactly where I was.

The Maury River was to my right, and I was standing in the old lock that had been built as part of a waterway to help get goods from Richmond up over the Appalachians. I'd come here at least twice for school field trips, and Mom and I packed a picnic on sunny days and sat by the river just behind me. *The Ben Salem Lock that was part of the James and Kanawha Canal.* Never thought it would be helpful that I knew that tidbit of info.

At least this time, I wasn't lost. I was miles from home without my phone or shoes, but I knew where I was, and that was better than the last time. And I still had my cheese doodles, so there was that.

This time, I also knew what was happening. I knew I needed to pay attention. I knew I needed to touch something, something significant. It was my skin on something that would let me see. So I set down my cheese doodles and started wandering around and putting my hand against the big stones of the lock walls. *Nothing.*

I wandered around the corner and touched the lower walls but still nothing. I methodically went through and put my hand on every stone there, noticing the feathering marks from where people—probably enslaved people—had chiseled the stones apart. I imagined the men cutting these huge rocks with hammers and pieces of wood jammed into hand-drilled holes. I pictured them lifting the stones into place—their dark hands rough and strong. I knew enough about this lock and about slavery to know it wasn't white folks who had built this thing.

But still, no matter what I touched, nothing. I wandered over, looked across the river, and peered up and down to see if anybody was fishing out there today. I was completely alone except for the cars whizzing by behind me.

I needed to think, so I sat back against a sycamore tree by the river. It took me a few minutes to decide that my best course of action was to walk up the road to the Coffee Pot and ask if I could use their phone, and I was just about to head out when I saw them. The soles of two black feet hanging just above my head.

I screamed.

I jumped up and took a bunch of stumbling steps back when I almost bumped into the feet. There, hanging from the tree, was the body of a woman. Her head was tilted to one side, and her eyes were closed. I stared, I'm ashamed to say. I had never seen a dead body before, especially not dead by lynching. That's what this was. Clearly. This woman had been lynched.

As I stared, I began to see the woman more clearly. She looked young, and even though her face was distorted from her terrible death, she looked kind. She was wearing a simple burgundy dress with little pink flowers on it. Her feet were bare, and her hair was slipping loose from a bun at the back of her head. Her body was swinging slightly in the nonexistent breeze.

I felt my knees give way finally, the shock setting in, and that's when I saw another woman standing on the other side of the tree, her back to the woman hanging. Her shoulders were shaking with sobs. This was who I was here to see: this dead woman grieving another dead woman.

I took a deep, steadying breath, got to my feet, and walked over to the crying woman. I laid a hand on her shoulder. She jumped back and raised her hands toward her face as if to fend off a blow.

"It's okay," I said as softly as I could. "My name's Mary." All sorts of things came through my head. I wanted to say I was there to help, but help with what? I wanted to tell her it would be okay, but clearly, it wouldn't be. A woman was hanging in a tree. So instead, I just sat down and hoped she'd sit too.

Eventually she did, a few feet away, but squarely facing me as if to keep an eye on me . . . or to keep me from sneaking up on her. She took a few deep breaths and said, "You can see me?"

"Yes. I can see you." My eyes must have trailed to the tree.

"You can see my mama, too?"

2

I walked over to the young woman and sat down near —but not touching—her. She looked like she needed some space . . . although I wondered how that was possible since this woman had probably been alone for decades. Still, grief is not a simple thing. . . . I had learned that over the past couple of years.

"Yes, I can see the woman in the tree. She's your mom?"

"Yes. They killed her, missus. They killed her."

I forced myself to look up at the hanging woman's face. "It's horrible. I'm so sorry." The words felt limp and weak in the air.

"Said she stole flour from the general store over in Terra Linda."

I knew the store she was talking about. It sold antiques and scented candles now, but they still used a lot of the old fixtures from back when the shop carried everything from nails to candy to, apparently, flour. "Flour? How does someone steal flour?"

"Exactly what I said, missus. It's not like she could scoop it up in her hands and walk out with it now, is it?" The woman's voice was getting sharper, brighter.

"Right. Ridiculous."

The young woman looked me dead in the eyes. "You believe

me?" She leaned toward me just a bit, her forehead lowering to the level of my eyes. "You believe she innocent?"

From my previous experience with ghosts, I'd learned that black people get accused—and convicted without trial—for crimes that had never happened. Couple that experience with the twenty-first century truths of police brutality and white people calling the cops on black folks for trying to go into their own apartment or for swimming in their community pool, and I found myself almost always believing the black person in a situation of violence just as an act of resistance to the doubt that seemed to trail black people in every story. I nodded.

The young woman leaned back and looked at me. Her gaze was softer now, but no less intense. "Missus, forgive me for asking, but who are you?"

"I'm Mary. Mary Steele. I'm from just over the hill there."

She continued to look me dead in the eye. "And you here because?"

"That's a long story. I will tell you sometime though. Do you mind if I ask your name?"

"I'm Sarah. Sarah Jennings, missus. We live back there in Wildy Hollow. You know it?"

I didn't, but I could see where she was pointing: back toward Terra Linda, my town, and up into the hills. "Sort of. And your mom? What was your mom's name?

"Beverly. But everybody called her Bo." She paused and turned to look at the river. "Don't quite know why they called her that except that everybody up the hollow is called something or other."

I could see her almost smile with memory and belonging-ness. But then, she must have seen her mother's feet up behind me because the tears sprung to her eyes again.

"When did this happen, Sarah?" I asked quietly, knowing the answer was complicated by time and memory and the way this thing—whatever it was that I could do—was.

"Last night." She looked me in the eyes. "Last night ninety years ago."

1928. I had some vague notion of women in high-waisted dresses and Model Ts when I thought of the 1920s. But in this context, the context where people were killed for supposedly stealing flour, I had nothing. I couldn't even remember a movie I'd seen or a TV show set in the 1920s that included black people unless they were maids or butlers.

"So you can see me?" Sarah circled back to her original question.

"Yes." I paused. I never knew how to explain this to anyone, living or dead. "I don't know why or how. It's happened before though." She looked interested—or maybe she just had nothing else to do—so I told her about the two other times I'd seen ghosts. By the end of what was a far longer story than I'd thought it would be going in, her brow had furrowed.

"You only see the ghosts of black folks then?"

I hadn't thought about it that way before, but it was true. I'd never seen a dead white person, that was for sure. "Yeah, I guess that's right."

"Don't you think it's strange that a white girl would see dead black people?"

Now that she put it that way . . . "I guess so. You believe me though?"

"I do. But still . . ."

She didn't look upset, just quizzical, and I felt the same way. I knew why I'd seen Moses; the fact that he was my ancestor made that pretty clear. But then why Charlotte a few months back? She wasn't my kin. And why Sarah now?

Sarah and I sat staring out at the Maury River for a few minutes in silence, a comfortable, easy silence, before she said, "Can I ask you another question?"

"Sure." I turned my body back to face her.

"Why do you think they lynched my mama here?"

I looked around again. The lock would have been much

cleaner, maybe still in use, in 1928. I knew from those field trips that the lock had been built around 1840, so it was old even then. Maybe that had something to do with why Beverly Jennings had been hanged here . . . but somehow that didn't seem right.

"SARAH, when you were alive, how big was this road?" I gestured behind us at the four-lane highway running between the base of the mountains and the river.

"Well, not that big." She looked over at the highway. "But big enough for two wagons to pass." I figured the road had long been a cut through in the mountains from Terra Linda to Lexington. There weren't many easy places to move through the mountains.

"So maybe that's it. Maybe they wanted people to see . . ." I didn't stop myself soon enough.

Sarah's face clouded over, and she stared out at the water again. "Yeah, maybe." Her voice was almost a whisper.

A less comfortable silence settled down over us. I watched this girl—about my age, maybe a little older—from the corner of my eye. She had on a simple dress that was cinched just a bit at the waist. She was barefoot like me and like her mama. And her hair was pulled back into a tight bun at the top of her head. Her skin was the color of walnut bark, and she had this small mole just below her left eye. She was beautiful in a simple, unfussy way.

Then, I turned to look at her. "Sarah, how did you die?"

3

*S*arah turned to look at me then shrugged her shoulders. "Oh, I was shot."

She said this like it was no big deal. I was speechless. To be shot means—at least most of the time—that someone pointed a weapon, a weapon they had to load with a bullet with the intention of doing injury to someone or something, at you and then pulled a trigger. This seemed to warrant more than a shrug.

I recovered my tongue and said, "What! Who shot you?"

"The men that hanged my mama." She stood and started to walk a few steps away.

"Wait! Why did they shoot you?" I hurried to her side. "Did they claim you tried to steal something, too?"

"Oh no, they shot me because I came at them with a knife when I saw they'd lynched Mama. They had reason to shoot me." She walked closer to the river. "They glad they did, too, or they'd be the dead ones."

I felt heat flush my neck. I didn't like talk of violence, even when I understood the reasons behind it. It made me uncomfortable. I wanted people to just be civil, to be kind. Even though I'd seen people try to bulldoze gravestones, burn down schools, and intimidate teenagers all to cover up their own hatred, I still wanted to see people as mostly good. I knew I was being naïve, but I was pretty okay with that.

But then, I saw Sarah glance back at her mother, and I dropped my head. Who was I to call for gentleness in the face of such violence? Who was I to judge? I scuffed my bare heel into a patch of grass.

Sarah had walked a bit further on toward a big boulder a few feet further along the river's edge, and now she leaned back against the stone. I made my way over to her and leaned beside her. The rock was warm on my back, and I realized that the air had begun to chill as the sun dropped behind the mountains around us. I'd need to figure out how to get home soon.

"How old are you?" Sarah's voice broke my silence.

"Seventeen. You?"

"Same. You go to school?"

"YEP, ELEVENTH GRADE." I paused. "Everybody goes to school through twelfth grade at the same school in Terra Linda now." Back when Sarah had been alive, she probably had already done all the years of school she could in a school for black kids, maybe at a Rosenwald School for rural black kids like the one where Charlotte taught. Maybe through eighth grade or so.

"That's good. I guess. Everybody get along?" She was staring out across the river at the hill just beyond where the sycamore leaves were starting to leaf out.

"Mostly," I said. "Better than it used to be." I felt sure of that statement.

She looked at me then. "It'd have to be, wouldn't it? Couldn't hardly be worse."

Again, she had a point. We sat still for a moment longer, and then I said something I never thought I'd need to say. "Do you want me to help you cut your mother down? From that tree, I mean?"

Sarah squinted just a bit and leaned toward me. "Yes."

So we stood up and made our way back to the tree. I felt in my pockets for the pocketknife I often wished I carried like the boys around here, but I had nothing but a couple of dollar bills and a wrapper from a Caramel Cream that I'd eaten on the way home from school. Sarah looked at a loss too.

Then, I saw my bowl full of cheese doodles back over by the lock. It was one of Mom's good bowls. Light-green "stoneware," she called it. Heavy. I made my way over and dumped the doodles on the ground, knowing I'd be the biggest hero of birds nearby. Then, I strolled over to the lock wall and threw the bowl against it.

The bowl broke into a bunch of pieces, and I selected one large triangle with a sharp edge. Sarah nodded, and I put the shard in the front pocket of my jeans and began to climb. Never had I been more grateful for those big trees in the churchyard and all the times I'd hidden during Vacation Bible School evenings.

I could hear Sarah climbing up behind me, her bare legs rasping against the tree trunk. We carefully climbed out onto the limb, and I watched Sarah wrap her legs over the tree branch like it was part of a set of monkey bars. Then, she lowered her body down so that her hands reached under her mother's arms. I carefully tucked Sarah's dress between her knees—I was the only one who could see her, but still, a girl deserves some decorum—and began to saw at the rope.

It only took a few minutes before the thick cord gave way, and I heard Sarah grunt as the weight of her mother's body shifted to her arms. I scrambled quick as I could over Sarah's legs and back down the trunk so that Sarah could lower Bo's legs into my arms. The woman weighed more than I thought she would, and I almost dropped her. But I was not going to let that happen, so I stiffened my arms and widened my stance as I braced Bo's belly against my face. When Sarah got down, I let her mother's upper body fall into her waiting arms.

Then, I walked away as the daughter cradled her mother and sobbed.

I didn't know what to do. Was it even possible to bury a ghost body? And if so, how? I was pretty sure we couldn't dig a body-sized hole with a shard of green bowl. But I couldn't just leave Sarah there with her mom's corpse. So I did something I'd only ever seen in movies—I gathered the branches that had fallen in the late-summer storms and laid them side by side. Then, I pulled down a big grapevine that had climbed up the lock walls. I did my best to lash the logs together with the vines and made a body-sized raft.

At some point, Sarah came over to help, leaving Bo's body leaning against the boulder. She looked almost as if she could have been taking a quiet spring nap there in the sun.

WHEN THE RAFT WAS READY, we carried Bo over and laid her gently on the logs. Then, we lifted the raft between us and took it down the slippery slope of grass to the river. I offered to say a prayer, but Sarah said, "No. God knows what I'm feeling. He knows my mama. No need to put words to it." I gave her a steady gaze then, looking to see if she were just being bitter and might regret that choice, but she seemed fine with it, solid. Still.

She gave the raft a gentle shove, and we watched her mother's body float down the Maury River, back toward Terra Linda, her home.

4

"I have to go," I said to Sarah a few minutes after the raft floated out of sight.

It's never easy for me to walk away from someone I know is alone . . . even if that someone is dead and has been alone for decades. Still, I knew my mother would be—if she hadn't already—coming out of her office when she finished meeting her therapy clients for the day, and I knew she'd be worried about me when she didn't find me at home.

Sarah just looked at me and nodded. Then, she walked over, leaned against the boulder, and put her head in her hands.

I felt like a jerk. But it was either leave this ghost behind or cause my mother worry. I was going to be a jerk to someone, so it might as well be the someone who wasn't going to lecture me over dinner.

I walked toward the Coffee Pot that was, in its most recent incarnation, a canoe rental shop. I hoped that even in the off-season someone at the shop might let me use the phone. I kept my eyes on my feet so I could avoid all the broken glass on the side of the highway and promised myself that I'd keep my phone and shoes on me at all times. I couldn't keep showing up places without shoes or a means to get help; it was ridiculous.

After I called Javier, I exhausted my extremely limited small talk about canoeing and rivers within thirty seconds, but the shop owner was a chatty sort and didn't seem to notice. I had learned more about portage and canoe safety than I really needed to know. So I was thrilled to see Javier's Nissan pull into the gravel parking lot outside a few minutes later. I thanked the shop owner for the use of her phone and picked my way carefully across the stones.

"You should really keep your shoes on all the time," my boyfriend said as I sat down.

Javier had been through this process with me twice before, and he still loved me—or at least I think he loved me. We hadn't really said that to each other, but I certainly felt that way.

I gave him my best eye roll as I slammed the car door. "Funny. Funny. Thanks for coming."

He gave me a sideways grin and headed toward home. "So who was it this time?"

"Sarah." I took a deep breath. "Her mother had been lynched at the boat lock." We were driving by those stone walls at that moment, and I could see Sarah still there against the boulder. She was staring out across the river. At least it looked like she'd stopped crying.

"Lynched? As in really lynched?" Javier's jaw clenched tight.

"Yes. I helped her cut her mother down."

"Oh, Mary." His hand found mine in my lap. "I'm so sorry."

"Yeah." I took a deep breath. "This one is really brutal, not that Moses's or Charlotte's experiences were any less awful. But to see someone hanged . . ." I couldn't really put words to it yet, and I didn't want to cry, so I stopped talking and stared out the windshield.

We rode in silence until we came to my road. "So should I text everyone to come over while you fill your mom in?"

This guy. He always knew. Always had the right thing to say. "Do you mind?"

"Nope. I'm on it." He parked his car behind my mom's, and I

hopped out. "Thirty minutes enough time? I'll go get us some pizzas."

Did I mention I loved this guy? "Perfect." I leaned back into the car and kissed him. "Thank you."

He smiled and put the car in reverse.

Mom was at the kitchen table when I came in, and she didn't look happy. I started to brace myself, but a second glance at her face told me she wasn't angry. I'd call her look, "Begrudgingly Resigned."

I grabbed a mug and filled it with hot water before scooping eight (no more, no less) spoonfuls of hot cocoa mix into it. Then, I sat down and waited.

It only took her a few moments and a deep breath before she asked, "Again?"

"Again. This time, I was over at the canal lock on 60. You know, where we picnic sometimes?"

The wrinkle just above her nose got deeper. "That's an odd place. I wouldn't imagine too many people spent too much time there. Unless there was a lock keeper or something?"

I took a sip of my cocoa. "Nope. A woman named Beverly Jennings was lynched there. But she wasn't alive, um, you know what I mean. It was just her ghost body. . . ." I couldn't really make sense of this myself. Ghosts don't really have bodies, but then Bo's body had been there. . . . I took a deep breath. "Her daughter Sarah was there, though." I told Mom about Bo's murder and Sarah's too, about cutting down Bo's body, about the raft. Mom listened. She's the best listener I know, even better than Javier.

"Okay, so the metaphysics of how one person's spirit can be alive and one person's body be dead but present and her spirit gone aside . . . why do you think you were there?"

I blew air hard out of my lips. "I have no idea. But everyone is coming over in a few minutes to see if we can't figure that out. Javier went to get pizza."

"Okay, sounds good. I'm going to get out of this skirt and

into yoga pants. Maybe you want to put on some shoes, just in case."

"All of you think you are so funny." But I laughed, and that felt good. I hadn't realized how tense I was until I felt the laugh loosen my shoulders.

It didn't last long though. I felt the threads of my neck pull taut again as I tried to imagine exactly what I was going to have to do to get justice for a lynched woman and her daughter.

5

*I*saiah had already been planning to come over for dinner, so he arrived first. Mom gave him a kiss on the cheek and then filled him in while I dug out the paper plates and leftover Valentine's Day napkins from the sideboard in the dining room. No one was going to want to wash dishes after this conversation.

JAVIER ARRIVED SOON after with four pizzas, of which I was sure he'd eat one himself. Marcie and Nicole, my two best friends and the cutest couple in school—after Javier and I, of course—came in just after he did, and Mr. Meade, our history teacher, still in his tie from school, showed up at the same time as our friend Shamila Jones from the Terra Linda Historical Society. Beatrice arrived last—it was always helpful to have a reporter around when you needed to spread the word or stir things up a bit.

THE GANG'S ALL HERE, I thought as everyone found a seat on the furniture or floor in the living room. Isaiah had lit a fire in the fireplace, and if you didn't know what we were here to talk about, you might have thought this was a scene from one of those Hallmark movies that take place in a small town just before a flower festival.

I HAD JUST FINISHED my first piece of pepperoni with extra cheese and cleared my throat to fill everyone in when there was a knock at the door. Mom shot me a look, and I turned to Javier, who kept eating. Officer Stephen Douglas stood at the door, and I saw Mom visibly relax. We'd had enough trouble with unwanted visitors in the past when it came to my ghost sightings, so I couldn't blame her for being a little on edge. But Stephen was a friend, and I was glad to see him.

"THOUGHT IT MIGHT BE useful to have him here since, well, you know," Javier said between bites.

I DID KNOW. There really is no statute of limitations on murder—the TV shows do get that right—and we might be looking at the need for law enforcement involvement. Not all the cops in this town were my biggest fans, but Stephen was a good person.

"ALRIGHT. I'm not sure exactly what Javier told you to get you all here, but I imagine it involved the words *Mary* and *ghost*, right?"
Everyone smiled. We'd done this before.

"WELL, this time, things are little odder than the usual, if that's even possible." I told them about the lock, about Beverly and Sarah Jennings, about how they died.

. . .

"So both women are dead," Marcie said. "But Bo is more dead than Sarah. Am I getting that right?"

"Yep. Sure are," I said. "I don't even want to pretend I understand it."

Mr. Meade swallowed a swig of Pepsi and said, "I've been studying up on the history of ghosts a bit for our local history unit in class."

I loved how Mr. Meade always worked fun stuff into his classes, and his way of talking about local history by presenting slideshows about people who supposedly still walked the places we knew—it was awesome. "And it seems that there are different kinds of hauntings. Some of them involve animate ghosts, that would be Sarah, and some of them have human figures that are more like set dressings—no offense—than actual people. Maybe that's the case with Beverly Jennings, with Bo." He looked at me as if I had an answer.

I just tilted my head and stared right back. I didn't even know how I showed up at the places where ghosts were much less why some ghosts could talk and move and some couldn't. I hadn't even met one of the "couldn't talk" kind before. I put my hands in the air and shrugged my shoulders. "Who knows?"

"Maybe this just means that Sarah is the one you are supposed to be helping," Nicole suggested. "I mean—"

And then, in the time it took me to blink my eyes, I was at the boat lock again, knee deep in water again, barefooted again. *Seri-*

ously, when would I learn? It took me even longer than usual to get my bearings because I had never . . . Transported? Ported? Portaled? Materialized? I'd never had *this thing* happen to me when I was with other people, so as much as it is always a surprise to show up somewhere else, I was even less prepared this time.

AT LEAST SOMEONE *will come get me,* I thought as I climbed out of the lock and headed toward the sycamore. Years of growing up in the country had equipped me with a sort of night vision, and the moon was almost full. So I could see at least enough to make it to the tree without falling. Sarah was sitting there, back to the trunk.

"HI," I said, plopping down next to her. "How are you?"

SARAH GAVE me some epic side-eye, and I felt the blood rush to my face. She'd just sent her mother's body down the river on a raft. How did I think she was?

"Right," I said and leaned back against the tree. "So I told some friends about what happened to your mom. I expect they'll be here soon. Just so you know."

SARAH LEANED FORWARD and faced me. "Okay. Doesn't matter, I guess." She rubbed her face with her hands and let out a long slow breath.

WE SAT for several minutes by that moonlit river, the streams of the car headlights waving over our heads from the highway. I listened to the water run over the rocks of its bed and hoped. . . .

I don't know what I hoped for exactly. For peace, maybe. For answers. For justice.

WHEN THE CARS full of my friends pulled up, Sarah stood, straightened her dress, and took my hand. I felt the soft dryness of her skin against mine and breathed a silent prayer: "Lord, have mercy. Lord, bring justice. Lord, help me."

$\mathcal{I}$ knew that when my friends got out of the cars, they would see Sarah. That's what happened when I touched a ghost—they became visible to others. I needed to prepare Sarah.

"They're going to be able to see you." I held up our hands and nodded. "Okay?"

She let out a long breath. "Okay."

I took another look at our joined hands and felt my chest tighten a bit. It wasn't very common, even in the twenty-first century, to see black and white people holding hands, and certainly, in the days of Sarah's breathing life, it had been absolutely forbidden. So for her to take my hand . . . it was an honor. It was a sign of trust that I had not yet earned and I expected was hard-given for a woman who had watched white people kill her mother. I looked up and to the right because I'd read somewhere that would stop you from crying.

Nicole's Subaru arrived first, and Marcie and Nicole climbed out. As they walked over, they instinctively grabbed each other's hands, and I saw Sarah's eyebrows raise just a hair. But then, she looked each woman in the eye and said, "I'm Sarah. How do you do?"

One by one, my friends introduced themselves, each offering their hands for her to shake. With each introduction, I saw a sort of light grow in Sarah's face. I wouldn't know until later that it wasn't just that she was in awe that so many people could see her again, but it was more that so many white people actually saw *her*. As we made our way over to a picnic table, she whispered, "You got black people as friends? That Mexican guy and an oriental girl, too?"

I nodded, and she shook her head and smiled. I felt the corners of my mouth turn up.

Marcie and Javier dragged another table from the other side of the meadow. Mom set a couple of electric lanterns out—of course, she had come prepared. And Mr. Meade and Beatrice pulled thermoses and Styrofoam cups out of their satchels and began passing hot cups of cocoa to everyone. Each time a cup passed through Sarah's hands, I saw her lean in to smell.

Isaiah sat on the end of the table, legs folded awkwardly in front of him, and said, "So Sarah, Mary told us about your mom. We are all so sorry."

Everyone nodded, and Beatrice put her arm around the young woman's shoulder. I saw Sarah shift a little closer into Beatrice's body.

"On the way over, I looked to see if I could find any information about your mother's murder," Shamila said.

Sarah interrupted. "Oh, my mama wasn't murdered."

Everyone looked at me, but then Mom spoke, "Sarah, Mary said your mother was lynched."

"That's right."

"Well, lynching is murder," Mom said quietly.

Sarah looked at Mom then at me before letting her eyes take in the nods of everyone at the table before letting her eyes drop to her hands. "Not where I come from."

I didn't even know what to make of this. How was it even possible for someone to believe what had happened to Beverly Jennings was anything but the most horrible of crimes. "What do you mean, Sarah? How can what happened to your mom not be murder?"

She looked at me and tilted her head. "Murder, as I know it, is something illegal. It ain't illegal to lynch someone for a crime."

My mind flashed to the faces from the news: Sandra Brand, Freddie Gray, Trayvon Martin, and I felt like someone had clobbered me with a sledgehammer. Those murders hadn't been illegal either. I couldn't stop the tears this time.

"Well, here it is." I felt Shamila's words as much as heard them.

Sarah looked up again, and tears sat in the bottom of her eyes. She nodded slowly.

Shamila continued. "I did find that the newspaper ran a story about your mother's death . . . with pictures. Horrible pictures." She passed her phone around the table, and each person's face blanched as they glanced at the screen.

When the phone reached me, I saw Bo's body, exactly the way she'd looked when I had first arrived, except the trees around the lock and all the meadow were full of white people, even children. One little boy had a lollipop in his hand. It looked like so many of those photos of lynching I'd seen before, but it still unsettled me. I felt angry and distraught and sorrowful all at the same time.

When the phone came to Sarah, she studied the strange, glowing device in her hand, glanced at the picture, and passed it on. "Yes, that's what happened a few hours ago. They was probably a hundred people here to watch. They sent around flyers. That's how I knew they'd be here then, why I come to save my mama or get revenge for her one."

Javier's voice was loud, too loud. "They passed out flyers to announce a lynching!" I laid my hand over his as I felt the rage edging everything aside inside me again. But that voice of church and all that Bible reading rose at the back of my throat: "Vengeance is mine, saith the Lord." The rage eased back, but then I just felt queasy.

"I would have done the same thing," Marcie said, and I turned to look at my best friend. She stared right at me. "They killed her mother, Mary," my friend explained softly.

I looked across the table at my mom and suddenly felt that rage grow big and red and pointed. I didn't try to curb it. I let it come to my mouth, and it tasted like venom. If someone had come after my mom and threatened her, I would have done more than grab a knife.

Sarah was looking over at the sycamore when I was finally able to turn my attention away from myself. "I was too late, though. They'd already tied her up. The horse had already started running."

I could picture the scene. Bo standing on a horse's back, balancing herself on her tiptoes. A smack on the horse. A hard drop. A round of applause, . . . and Sarah there at the edge of the road, butcher knife in a hand clenched so tight her knuckles were white.

"I didn't even think. I just charged at the man holding the horse, and I almost got to him. Almost got my knife to his chest when I felt the burning in my stomach and looked down to see blood. The man with the horse looked at me as I fell to the ground and then walked over to the boulder, mounted, and rode away. I could see other people stepping around me as they made their way to the road."

Javier squeezed my hand, and I could hear him sniffle. Even Stephen looked on the verge of tears.

Beatrice tugged Sarah tight against her. "I'm sorry, child. I'm so sorry."

Sarah looked up at me and smiled, a tiny, tight smile. I smiled back as I wiped a tear away.

We sat silently for a few minutes until Mr. Meade spoke. "Forgive me for sounding insensitive," he said, "but, Sarah, did you say you had a knife?"

"Yessir, I did."

"Do you still have it?" the teacher asked.

"No, sir. A little boy came over and took it out of my hand before I died."

We all looked at one another and then back at Sarah. "A white little boy?" Marcie asked.

"Yep. Johnny Tucker. I knew him from the store in town. His daddy owned the place."

I felt a shiver pass through me. The now-antique store still said "Tucker's General Store" above the door. And I knew the Tuckers. They didn't own the building anymore—at least I didn't think they did—but John Tucker Jr. was the mayor in town. His daddy was John Tucker Sr.

Mom caught my eye. "How old was Johnny, do you think, Sarah?"

Sarah wrinkled her nose and looked up to her right. "Probably eight or nine, I suppose." Then she squinted a bit and looked at my mom. "Why you askin'?"

Mom took a deep breath and looked at Sarah close. "Because, Sarah, that little boy who took your knife? He's still alive."

Sarah rocked back a bit and looked toward the river again and shook her head. "That rotten kid still living and my mama floating down the river. Ain't that something!"

I could see tears pooling in Sarah's eyes again, but I didn't think it was sadness this time. Something about the set of her jaw told me this was anger brimming forth. I didn't blame her. I was still feeling pretty pissed off myself.

Nicole and Javier jumped to their feet, and I almost followed them. I knew where we were headed: to get some answers from Old Man Tucker.

But Isaiah's next words stopped me cold. "Why'd Tucker take your knife, Sarah?"

She looked back from the river and met Isaiah's gaze. "I figure he wanted a souvenir of what his lying tongue had done."

"You mean . . ." My words trailed off.

Sarah was looking back across the river again. "He's the one accused my mama of stealing that flour."

7

*N*one of us knew quite what to say to that, and Sarah looked like she could use a rest. So we said good night, told her we'd be back tomorrow, and headed to our homes. I rode with Mom back over the mountain to our house because I didn't know what to say, and as good as Javier was to me, I knew he'd need quiet to think about all this. I am not a person who does "quiet" when things upset me. Mom says I'm a verbal processor. I just know I need to talk it out to figure it out.

The whole ride home, I repeated what had happened that day, and when it came to talk about Old Man Tucker, I worked my way around him in words. "Hard to imagine him as a little boy."

Mom nodded.

"But little kids do lie, I guess. Maybe he thought it was funny?"

I looked over at Mom, who was still silent, but her mouth had slid to the side, a sure sign she didn't agree with that idea.

"Or maybe he had something against Bo?"

Still that squinty mouth.

I turned to look out the window beside me and watched the bright-green of the new leaves against the dark of night. I tried to remember when I was seven. Second grade. Stevie Murray. My first boyfriend. I had gotten in big trouble for holding his hand during reading time, and I'd known I would. Mom had told me that girlfriend-boyfriend stuff was not for class. I'd known better when I was seven.

So Johnny Tucker had known better. So he'd had a reason for lying about Sarah's mom.

"Maybe he was mad at Sarah's mama?"

Mom's lips untwisted a bit.

"Maybe she'd gotten him in trouble for something."

A little less twist.

"Maybe . . ." I paused and took a deep breath. "Maybe he didn't like getting in trouble because of something a black woman said."

Mom let out a long sigh. Clearly, she and I were now thinking the same thing.

"But if his parents knew that there was history . . ."

Mom's car pulled into our driveway, and she turned off the ignition and looked at me. "Don't be naïve, Mary."

I felt rage course down through my fingers. "His parents knew he was lying but let people believe he was telling the truth!"

"Aren't many parents I know who don't figure out pretty quick when their kids are telling stories."

"Those bas—"

"Mary Olivia Steele!"

I lowered my head. Mom had no patience for swearing, even with cause.

That night, as I tried to fall asleep, I thought of all the seven-year-olds I knew. The kids from church. The neighbors. I tried to picture those sweet little faces and the way they always wanted me to do stuff with them: take a walk, hang out in their tree-houses, play a game. I tried to imagine any one of them being hateful enough to tell a really ugly lie about someone they simply didn't like.

I was having a hard time picturing it until I remembered Bonita Ramirez. Bonita had been in my second-grade class. She had long brown braids that reached down to her butt, and she spoke English with a Spanish accent because her family was from Mexico. She was smart, and she raised her hand to answer questions in class all the time. But every time she did, one of our classmates would say, "Phew, put your arm down. I can smell you from all the way over here." Bonita's face would get red, but she'd keep her arm up. I admired her for that.

One day, I'd heard Bonita crying in a bathroom stall. She had been very quiet, but it's pretty easy to tell when someone is sniffling in the echo chamber of an all-tile room. I waited until she came out because I'd had my own times crying in the bathroom and had always wished someone would wait to ask me if I were okay. But when I asked Bonita, she just smiled and said, "Thank you, Mary. I'm okay," and walked out.

I came home and told Mom what was happening. She sat me down at the table. "Where is Bonita from, Mary?"

"Mexico. Her parents are here to help over at Slater's Farm." Bonita had told us all that when she'd introduced herself to the class on the first day. "But she lived in North Carolina before this. They worked to pick watermelons there."

"Ah, so they are migrant workers. Hard workers for sure." Mom took a deep breath. "You know that not all people like people who come from other places, don't you, Mary?"

I'd furrowed my brow and looked at Mom more closely. "You mean people don't like Bonita because her family is from Mexico?"

"Maybe. Sometimes that happens. It's kind of like the way someone people don't like your friend Marcie because she has dark-brown skin."

"But that's wrong, Mom! We're supposed to like somebody or not because of how they act, not what they look like." I looked hard at my mom. "Or where they are from, right?"

"Right, Mary. But not everybody is as kind as you are. Some

people are really scared. They think that Bonita's family is coming to take their jobs or that Bonita's parents are here because they want free stuff."

I remember being so confused. "But Bonita wrote a story about her family, and she said they worked all the time—from the time the sun came up until it went back down. I don't know anybody else who has parents that work like that."

"Exactly. The things these people are scared of aren't real, Mary. They are excuses for them to act badly to people who look and talk differently than they do. These people are prejudiced. Do you know that word?"

I didn't, but Mom explained it to me so I could understand.

"But then why do my friends say Bonita stinks?"

"They are just being mean, repeating what their parents have taught them about people from Mexico. Sometimes, they might even call her names."

I thought about some of the things people called Bonita when she wasn't there. I hadn't realized until right then that they were mean. I'd just thought they described the fact that Bonita brought beans and rice for lunch most days.

The next day after Mom and I talked, someone had called Bonita a "Beaner" when she raised her hand to answer a question. I had felt my face flush and tears come to my eyes, like they always did when I was mad. But I hadn't said anything. I just sat there and watched Bonita hold her hand high until the teacher called her name.

As I drifted off to sleep that first night I'd met Sarah, I wished I had stood up for Bonita. I hadn't called her names or made fun of her . . . but I'd stayed silent, and that felt just as bad.

The next day at lunch, Marcie, Nicole, Javier, and I were pretty quiet. We'd gone through some through break-ups and bad grades—and two ghost encounters—together before, but something about this one felt heavier, harder. Maybe it was that Sarah was our age. Maybe it was the lynching.

"You know they just built that new lynching museum down

in Alabama?" Javier broke the silence at the table. "Mr. Meade was telling us about it this morning in U.S. history."

I'd jotted down some notes during the lecture because I felt like I needed to know more, but I wasn't sure where Javier was going with this idea.

"Well, what if we could get Beverly Jennings memorialized there? What if we could get a plaque with her name on it?"

Sometimes, this guy . . . as if I couldn't love him more. . . .

I took a deep breath. I had been worried all night about how to deal with Old Man Tucker, . . . and I knew we would have to come to that. But this sounded better, hard but easier. Less confrontational that forcing an old man to own up to what he witnessed and what his father did.

Nicole leaned forward quickly. "I love that idea. Do you know how we do that?" She looked at Javier.

"No clue. But I bet Mr. Meade does."

We rushed through Mr. Meade's door as soon as the final bell rang. I'd already texted Mom to let her know I was staying after to do some research, and she'd replied with a smiley emoji. She was embarrassingly emoji-obsessed; the woman could find more ways to justify the smiling pile of poop than anyone I knew.

"Whoa, folks." Mr. Meade said as we all started talking at once. "I appreciate the historical enthusiasm, but one at a time, please. What can I do for you?"

Everyone looked at me, and I felt my shoulders tighten a bit. This gift-curse thing came with a lot of responsibility. "Well, Javier mentioned the lynching memorial, and we wondered . . ."

Mr. Meade didn't even let me finish. "I've already started doing the research." He pulled a file out of his desk—Mr. Meade had a file for everything. "Shamila has already started gathering records. In fact, I'm heading over to meet her now. . . ."

He didn't even have to finish his sentence before we were on the way out the door. We were old hats at this research game by now, and I knew we'd all come to love the search for information, even when the information was hard to accept. It was like a big scavenger hunt that made me feel productive and smart and helpful all at once.

Terra Linda is a tiny town, so we all walked to the Historical Society's building together. The sun was out, and the leaves were starting to fill out and finally make shadows. As we strolled down Main Street, I felt a bit like the people on that black and white TV show in that town called Mayfield—no that's not it. Mayberry. The storefronts were all decorated for Easter, and everyone waved or said hello to us as we walked. It would be easy to think everything was always good here . . . if we didn't know way better than that.

Shamila was in the big meeting room, and one end of the long wooden table was already covered in paper. I smiled when I saw it—Shamila had her systems, and they all involved color-coded index cards. I laid my backpack in a chair and went to stand over the piles of documents. Newspaper articles from 1928 were spread across the bottom row.

"Colored Woman Arrested for Theft"

"Citizens Bring Justice for Thievery"

I wasn't surprised to see the photos of Ms. Jennings's body on the cover of the newspaper, not after the other images we'd seen, but it still horrified me, set me back on my heels a bit. How was this horror considered "justice?" How could a newspaper justify showing someone's body? Now, even on the law enforcement shows, they cut out any images of bodies, even those in body bags.

I took off my sweatshirt and went to sit at the other end of the table. I just couldn't look at Bo's body hanging there anymore.

Shamila emerged from the archive room just beyond the table. Her arms were full of files, and I knew she'd pulled everything about the lynching and everyone involved from the Historical Society records. The woman was the epitome of thorough.

She made three stacks beside me on the table, and I stood up to look. One was a pile of folders labeled with people's names—

Jennings and Tucker of course, but also Sanderson and Pope. The next pile was folders of police records from 1928, all labeled "Theft at Tucker Store." In the third stack, I could see the black and white edges of photographs. I immediately decided against starting there—too much unnoted bias—and instead, pulled the files with the peoples' names over to me.

"Shamila?" I held up the folders labeled with the names I didn't recognize as she turned from the whiteboard on which she'd begun writing names and dates. I couldn't help but think of the murder boards from all those police TV shows.

"Oh, right. So I pulled the files for any families whose names showed up in the captions of the newspaper photos." She smiled at me from the corner of her mouth. "You know me, I leave no stone unturned."

I grinned and started flipping through one of the folders marked "Jennings." Most of the documents were letters from one family member to another, probably donated to the Society over the years. I didn't see anything from a Beverly, Bo, or Sarah, but then I saw a photo of a family with the caption "The Jennings' Farm" and realized these Jennings were white—probably still kin to Sarah and her family—but that fact wasn't really relevant at this moment.

Two more folders of white Jennings later, and I finally came across a very slim folder with a photocopy of one of the newspaper articles that Shamila had pulled out onto the table.

Beverly Jennings, 33, was brought to justice by the law-abiding citizens of Terra Linda on Monday afternoon for the crime of stealing from Tucker's General Store. Jennings had been held in the county jail to await trial, but the good citizens of the town knew of her guilt and so spared the community an unwarranted expense and emotional travail. Several men, including Gilford Tucker, Dalfred Pope, and Bufort "Bucky" Sanderson, brought Jennings to the Ben Salem boat lock on Monday afternoon about 3 p.m. There, she was hanged for her crime while a good-sized crowd looked on. Sadly, Jennings's daughter Sarah, 16, went wild and threatened young Johnny Tucker with a knife and was killed by the boy's father. "We just hope," Gilford Tucker told this reporter, "that colored learn to do right and mind their place in this town so we don't have to make an example of anyone else."

I put the piece of paper back in the folder and laid the folder carefully down on the table. Then, I got up and walked out of the room. I needed air.

I passed Javier and Marcie as I left the building and heard Marcie say, "Give her a minute," as I let the door to the street close behind me. I just had to move my body, had to get the rage in my chest out into my limbs. "Make an example." It wasn't just that they killed Bo and Sarah; it was that they were showing the black people of Terra Linda that stepping out of line would not be tolerated in any way.

And the newspaper—it was lauding these people, treating them like heroes, as if they'd rescued some little girl's kitten rather than strung a woman's body up in a tree. I couldn't even begin to fathom that kind of openly hostile racism.

But I knew the kind that lived in my town today had come up against it too many times already. Only a year ago I would have said everyone in my town got along. I wanted to think it had been easier back then, when racism was so obvious, but that was just a lie people told ourselves to justify our lack of action today: "Racism is more subtle these days." I'd said that, too, but how could it be better that people could be lynched and then have their killers celebrated in the newspaper? That wasn't better, not at all.

Each time I thought of Bo's body or imagined Sarah's face, the rage rose up again, and I walked faster and faster. Before I knew it, I was at Tic Toc's burgers on the edge of town, and I was famished. I texted Javier to let him know where I was and then sat down at a booth by the window. I ordered a double cheeseburger, large fry, and a large Diet Coke. I needed fuel for this fire.

As I sipped my soda and watched for Javier's car, I heard the bell ring over the door behind me. Then, I saw someone walk past my booth to a stool at the counter. It was John Tucker Jr., the mayor. I felt all the blood rush out of my arms. This was the grandson of the man who killed Sarah, the son of the man who picked up Sarah's knife as a souvenir.

I looked down and saw my hand clenched around my fork so tightly that the handle was cutting into my palm. I slowly let the fork go and sat back against the bench. *Deep breaths, Mary. Deep breaths*

8

*B*y the time Javier arrived with Marcie and Nicole, I had managed to calm down enough that I didn't think I would actually stab Mayor Tucker, but I was giving him the meanest stare I could fashion.

"Girl, you better quit giving that man the stink eye. He is the mayor," Nicole said. "You don't need him giving you any trouble."

I pulled my eyes away and looked at my friends. They each seemed their own kind of worried, and I felt bad for, yet again, making them take care of me. "I'm fine." I let out a big puff of air. "Really. Did you see that article I was reading?"

"Shamila showed us," Javier said as he took my hand. "It made me angry too."

Nicole and Marcie nodded. "Us too."

"I just don't understand. . . ." But I couldn't put words to all the things that were impossibly nonsensical about this. I let my head drop onto my arms on the table.

"Double cheeseburger?"

I looked up to the waitress, who looked a bit worried herself. "That's mine. Thank you."

She set the platter in front of me and took orders from my

friends—more burgers and fries—before heading back behind the counter.

I made a huge pile of ketchup in the corner of my plate then shoved it to the center of the table. No one needed more of an invitation, and soon, my fries were mostly gone. Good thing we had three more orders coming. This was the kind of afternoon that required lots of fried food.

"We have documentation of the lynching—photos even, so Mr. Meade thinks we can get Ms. Jennings memorialized at the museum in Mississippi," Javier said between mouthfuls of fries. "And he thinks we should organize a soil-gathering ceremony at the lock, too?"

I stared at my boyfriend while I chewed a bite of my burger.

"Oh, right. You had gone for a walk when he told us. At the museum, they have a room where there are jars full of soil from lynching sites. We all thought it would be important to have some soil from Terra Linda there too."

I swallowed. "Definitely." I looked out the window. "But I don't know that I can do another big thing. I don't want to wake up with tombstones on my lawn again." My mind flashed back to those days after I'd just met Moses, to that other white man who really didn't want to accept the truth of history.

"Maybe I can help with that?" Mayor Tucker stood at the end of the table. "I hope you'll forgive me, but I couldn't help over-hearing what you were talking about. You're talking about a lynching here in Terra Linda?"

I felt like all the air had gone out of the room. He looked kind enough and actually a little shocked, but I didn't trust him, not after what his grandfather and father had done to Bo and Sarah.

Luckily, Marcie still had her wits about her. "Um, yes sir, Mayor Tucker. A woman named Beverly Jennings was lynched at the old boat lock on the river in 1928." She took a deep breath. "Her daughter Sarah was killed that same night when she showed up to try and stop the hanging."

Mayor Tucker shook his head. "So two people were actually lynched that night? How horrible!"

I looked to Javier, and he shook his head. "Two people, Mayor?"

"Well, it sounds like Mrs. Jennings was actually lynched, as in hung. But the term *lynching* can actually be used to refer to anyone who was killed in a racially-motivated event. Like Emmett Till. He wasn't actually hung, but he was certainly lynched."

I remembered the photos of the handsome black teenager with the round face that Mr. Meade had shown us in class. After those pictures, Mr. Meade had shown the images of Emmett Till's grossly-swollen, unrecognizable head after he had been beaten up and dropped in the river. Men had come to his uncle's house, kidnapped, and killed him for supposedly whistling at a white woman.

I looked up at the mayor and tried to keep the skepticism out of my face. "So you'd help us with the ceremony?" I almost whispered the question.

"Of course. We need to remember these horrible events as a way of making amends for what happened and for healing."

I furrowed my brow, not wanting to believe him, but I felt hope buoy just a little in my soul. I felt it ebb, though, because I knew we'd run into some real trouble if we didn't tell him the whole story.

"Mayor Tucker, I really appreciate your support in this, but I think there's something you need to know." My voice shook as I spoke.

The mayor met my gaze head on. "May I sit down?"

We nodded, and the mayor slid next to Javier in the booth.

"My grandfather had a part in that lynching. I know that."

I fought hard to keep my eyes on the mayor and not shoot my friends a *Can you believe this?* look.

"It's not a secret in our family. My dad still has a knife he picked up that day, says it belonged to the woman who was lynched, but I don't know how true that is. I was always just bothered by how proud he was to own it. He kept it mounted on the wall above the mantel in his basement." The mayor shook his head and ran a hand over his chin. "Horrible."

I put my hand under my jaw to keep my mouth from falling open, and Javier squeezed my knee hard under the table.

"So you don't have to worry about revealing a secret. Everyone in my family knows, and most of us are appalled. We'd like to do right by that family. We just haven't known how. Seems, though, that you have a way, and I'd like to support what you are doing."

I stared at Marcie, willing her not to say what I knew she was going to say. The woman had no filter.

"Mayor Tucker," she said, "Would you like to meet the family of the woman your grandfather murdered?"

I kicked my best friend hard under the table, and she shot me a look that said, *Shut up, Mary. I've got this.* I wasn't so sure she knew what she was doing, but the cat was out of the bag, so to speak, and it was racing up the road in front of us.

"You know her descendants? How?" He ran his hand down his face but then said without even a second's hesitation. "It doesn't matter. Yes, yes I would like to meet them. To say I'm sorry."

Marcie smiled, but I felt my blood go cold. I was going to have to tell the mayor I could see ghosts. That alone made my eyes hurt, but thinking about telling Sarah. I wasn't sure how she was going to take this.

Sometimes, in our desire to be helpful, we push too hard. I had learned this over the past few months. Often, we white people want so much to make things right, usually to ease our own discomfort, that we push our desires or ideas for how to make things better onto people of color. Marcie is black, so this wasn't a white person thing, . . . but it was a thing that we were doing without Sarah's permission, and I felt uneasy about that.

Was it really helping if we forced Sarah to confront the son of the man who killed her?

Still, the cat had torn out of the bag and run out of sight already, so we arranged to meet with Mayor Tucker the next day at the boat lock. He expressed some hesitation about the location because he didn't want to traumatize the descendants by bringing them to the place of the murder. But we assured him that they appreciated the opportunity to honor the site with this visit. . . . We conveniently forgot to mention that they didn't have any choice but to be there.

I was terrified about this meeting, terrified that the mayor would make my ability—I hated calling it that—public. I was terrified, too, that Sarah wouldn't be able to handle this meet-up, that we were forcing our agenda on her, that the mayor wouldn't be kind when he realized she was dead.

But I couldn't help but feel that little lift of hope again. Here was a man with power in our town, who was ready to make amends. Here was a tiny way forward. Maybe.

As we left the restaurant, and the mayor to his BBQ sandwich, I texted Mom to let her know we were headed to the lock to tell Sarah the mayor was coming the next day. Mom said that she and Isaiah would meet us there. I didn't know if we really needed a full-on meeting again, but I did know that telling my mom not to do something was not my wisest move . . . and also that it would not do any good anyway.

Sarah wasn't thrilled to see us when we got to the lock. But she wasn't unhappy either. I would say her mood was somewhere around melancholy, and I couldn't blame her. Ninety years of seeing your mother's body hanging in a tree had to be brutal, but then to watch that body, your only connection to her, now float down the river. I'd be downright distraught if I were her. But she was cordial, as always, which I knew was part of her home-training and part of the racism that she had lived in.

Everyone else sat around the still-assembled picnic tables, and I asked Sarah if we could take a walk. I didn't know exactly how far her tether that tied her to that spot would let her go, but I did know that she couldn't leave this spot. None of the ghosts I'd met could. I figured we could test out her range a bit. So we started down the bank of the river, she with her feet in the water, mine just at the edge.

"Sarah, John Tucker Jr. is coming here tomorrow."

She stopped. She didn't look up at me. She didn't walk away. She just stopped.

"I'm sorry we didn't ask you first. It just sort of happened." No need to throw Marcie under the bus here . . . although part of me wanted to absolve myself of this mistake.

Sarah started walking again. "Okay."

I watched her back as she moved away from me, too surprised to move. "So you're okay with this?"

"Well, what choice do I have? I can't leave, and apparently, he's coming here. So . . ."

"You do have a choice though. If I don't touch you while he's here, he won't be able to see you. You won't have to face him, or at least he won't know you're facing him."

She took a few more steps and then turned to me. "But you will have to face him. You will have to explain why you brought him, and you won't have no evidence for that. I don't want anybody else to get hurt, Mary. Not even a little." Her voice was really quiet. "Not nobody."

Tears sprung to my eyes. "Please, Sarah. Don't worry about me."

She gave me a gentle smile. "It's been so long since I had anyone to worry over. Let me."

Sometimes, when something true is said, when someone gives you a grace that stretches beyond what you can imagine, your heart cracks open. I felt mine widen there on that river's edge.

I reached out and hugged Sarah, and slowly, I felt her hands reach around my back and rest flat on my shoulder blades.

We joined the others at the picnic table, Sarah sitting close by my side. "Sarah is okay with Mayor Tucker coming," I said as I interlaced my fingers on the table. "But this isn't going to be easy." *For me*, I thought. "We need a plan."

By the time we left Sarah again—it never got easier to see her standing there alone—we had decided that we were first going to explain what we knew about the lynching from the newspaper articles to Mayor Tucker. Shamila began assembling a binder for the mayor when Isaiah gave her a call to fill her in.

Then, we were going to introduce him to Sarah. Mom would explain what had happened with Moses and Charlotte in the past months, and then I would touch Sarah. Then, we'd wait and see how he reacted.

If the mayor didn't run screaming or think we were playing a joke on him, Sarah said she'd like to sit and talk with him privately, but with me there. (There was that cracking in my heart again.) She wanted a chance to explain what really happened and to hear what he had to say. I thought this idea was so wise. Just the three of us meant we might all be more truthful. Too much of an audience makes anybody put on a performance.

Finally, if all went well, we'd talk about next steps, whatever those might be, and we'd let Sarah take the lead on what she wanted us to do, if anything, on her behalf. I was adamant about that, and everyone agreed. From the color in Marcie's cheeks, I could tell she was a little embarrassed about making this plan without talking to Sarah first. But we all live and learn.

The plan sounded good, and it felt right, respectful, honest. Still, I really doubted I'd be able to sleep that night. I was about to tell the mayor of my town that I could see ghosts. Glory day!

he next day at school flew by and also took about ninety-two hours. I was so excited and so nervous that I bit my nails way down past the quick. My friends didn't look much better when I saw them at lunch, and even Mr. Meade seemed a little edgy in sixth period.

But finally, the last bell rang, and we all piled into Marcie's Altima (the backseat of Javier's car wasn't exactly comfortable) and headed to the lock. The rest of the squad—Nicole had decided we were officially a squad—met us there, and Beatrice brought her reporters' notebook just in case we decided there was a story. Well, if Sarah decided she wanted us to tell the story.

Mayor Tucker was right on time, and Shamila gave him the full account of Beverly Jenning's lynching: from who was involved, including his grandfather, to Sarah's arrival to try and stop it, to the news coverage that glorified the murder. To his credit, the mayor looked good and chagrined, all the color gone from his face, and he sat with the binder Shamila handed him for a long time. I even saw him wipe his eyes a couple of times.

After a while, he stood up and came over to where I was standing by the sycamore. "Okay, I'm ready. Do you need to call them?"

I shook my head and turned my back to the mayor. No need for him to think I was talking to myself. "You still okay with this?" I whispered.

Sarah took a deep breath. "Yes. It's time."

I nodded and then placed my hand on her shoulder. I'd debated telling the mayor about what he was about to see, but I figured that would just raise up his skepticism and make it harder for him to believe. So I just went for it.

I heard him gasp. But then, he walked the few steps to us.

"Mayor Tucker, this is Sarah Jennings, the daughter of Beverly Jennings who was murdered here."

The mayor swallowed hard then put out his hand. "Nice to meet you, Miss Jennings." His voice caught. "I want to say I am so terribly sorry." I could see a million questions flashing behind the mayor's eyes, but he seemed to swallow them back and turn, instead, to the politeness all us Southerners had engrained.

I saw Sarah shudder just a bit, but then she grasped his hand with both of hers and said, "Thank you, Mr. Mayor. Thank you."

I let out a big sigh and felt the tension pass out of the air behind me. Introductions, between ghosts and living people, between black people and the white people who had harmed their families across history, are so hard, in every way. This one had one very well, even with all the pain still to sort.

Mom and everyone else walked casually toward the lock to give us some space, as Sarah had requested, and the three of us sat down at the picnic tables, Sarah still close enough that I could feel her shoulder against mine.

"Sarah, I know what my grandfather told me about that night, and Shamila gave me a good run down of things. But if you don't mind, I'd like to hear what happened from you, to hear the truth from someone who was there." The mayor's face was placid, still, a bit washed out. This was a lot.

I felt Sarah shift her weight and take a deep breath. "Well, sir, a bunch of men on horses came up to our house about three in the afternoon. My little brother, Joshua, had just come home from work. He was thirteen and worked at the furnace."

I pictured the squat, stone tower that was all that remained of the furnace today. It was just off the road on the way to our house.

"My daddy was still out at work at the furnace, so it was just me, Mama, and Joshua. When Mama heard the horses, she peeked out the window and told us to climb under the bed. 'Stay real quiet,' she said." Sarah's eyes disconnected from us as she talked, as if she were walking that day again.

"I could just see feet and hear voices. Mama said, 'Gentlemen, how can I help you?' in her best voice, the one she used with white folks, and a man said, 'Bo, you're under arrest for stealing.' I could see Mama's feet shifting, but her voice was steady. 'I'm sorry to hear that. May I know what I stole?'" Sarah smiled. "Mama was so smart with her words. She was sounding all polite, but I knew she was testing, making a stand."

I smiled and shivered. I loved Bo's spunk, but I knew it probably hadn't helped the situation.

"'Stealing flour from Tucker's Store. You need a sweater, Bo?' the man said, and Mama told him she'd be fine as she was. Then, she held her palm flat behind her hip to Joshua and me as she walked toward the door. We did as she said and stayed until we couldn't hear the hoof beats no more. Then, I took Joshua to our neighbor Farrow's place and asked her to keep him there while I did an errand. Miss Farrow didn't ask questions; she'd seen the horses and just put an arm around Joshua as she gave me a stern nod."

"Then, I walked to town, down to the jail, where I knew they'd taken Mama. I figured Miss Farrow would tell Daddy what happened when he got home and that he'd be down presently. But something told me to stay there. So stay I did. It didn't take long though."

I could see Sarah, just as she was at that picnic table, sitting on the low stone wall that still rims the courthouse and attached jail. We'd studied the buildings in history class because they'd been built back in the 1870s, when the town was first created. I'd sat on that same wall waiting for Javier or Marcie many an afternoon as they finished up a practice or rehearsal.

"Mr. Tucker," her eyes focused on the mayor for just a split second, "and Mr. Sanderson and Mr. Pope came up on their horses. They didn't pay me no mind and walked right into the jail. The sheriff was gone for the day, I figured, since he didn't stop them. Or maybe he just didn't care, because a few minutes later," she shook her head slowly, "out they came with Mama between them, her hands tied in front of her. She saw me there and gave her head a little shake, but I knew she wouldn't say nothing, too dangerous for me if they knew I was hers. They put her on the horse in front of Mr. Pope and rode out of town toward Lexington."

"I didn't know where they was headed until I heard a couple of white kids talking about the lock, about how everyone was going there to see the lynching of that . . ." she paused and looked at me, "of that nigger woman." Her breath shuddered.

I reached over and took her hand.

"I don't know what really came over me then. I just had to do something, so I ran into Tucker's store. Everybody was at the back by the nail boxes, talking about the lynching, so I just grabbed a big knife from the display on the counter and ran back out. Nobody called out after me, so I knew no one seen me." She paused and took a deep breath. "Don't that just beat all. I did steal from that store, and no one cared. But my mama, who wouldn't steal a breath from a fly, she gets strung up." Tears were sitting at the sills of her eyes.

The air was getting crisper around us, almost as if it knew what was coming, as if it was remembering. I squeezed Sarah's fingers tight for her comfort but also for mine.

"Someone had left a horse tied up in town, so for the second time in my life, I stole something, jumped on it, and headed for the lock. I'd never been there before—a white people's place it was—but I seen it plenty of times on the way to the movies in Lexington on the fifth Saturdays. Knew just where I was headed."

She let out a sigh that felt like it would shake the last of the new leaves off the trees.

"But I was too late. Mama was already dead there, in that tree. And all those white folks standing around sipping sodas and acting as if they was at the fair. I couldn't take it. I charged that horse right into that crowd and jumped off when I saw the men who took my mama. I would have killed them too. . . ."

The silence around us was heavy, and Mayor Tucker's face was red and sweaty. I waited, though. I'd learned that waiting often brought more than asking.

"Sarah, I don't know what to say." His voice was very quiet. "Nothing I *can* say really. I am so very sorry. There is nothing right about what happened. Not a thing." He paused and glanced up at the sycamore. "I would have done just what you did, or at least I like to think I would have. But then, maybe I would have been like my daddy, or worse, my granddaddy. Still, today, I am so very sorry."

Sarah gave him a good hard look with her soft brown eyes. She wasn't staring. No, she was studying, testing the truth of his words. After a few moments, she must have decided he was honest because she said, "Thank you, Mayor. Nothing you or I can do to change things, but you saying that, that's something."

Just then, I heard tires on the gravel parking area behind Sarah, and I and turned to see a big white Lincoln pull up. I put a soft hand on Sarah's arm, and then I was to my feet as fast as I could and saw Isaiah and Javier sprinting too. I didn't have time to explain to Sarah what was happening, but I could hear Mayor Tucker moving fast behind me toward the car.

His father was here.

hank goodness I reached the car first and was able to stand by the passenger side door when Johnny Tucker opened it. The old man had a reputation for being ornery, particularly to people of color—or "colored folks," as he called them. There was a lot of the word "boy" used at the local grocery store when a black cashier rang him up. I didn't want Isaiah or Javier to deal with that today.

"Mr. Tucker, it's nice to see you," I said in my most polite—and most fake—voice. "What brings you out here today?"

Mayor Tucker put his arm on my shoulder. "I believe that'd be my doing, Mary." He looked at me with eyes full of such sadness. "I mentioned to Daddy that I was coming out here today, and I guess you thought you'd come see what I was doing, sir?"

A white man about Mom's age came around the car then and opened the back door. He took a silver walker from the back seat and placed it between Johnny Tucker and me. The driver didn't look at me or anyone else, just helped Mr. Tucker stand up and then walked to the back of the car, where he lit a cigar and stood leaning against the trunk.

Johnny Tucker looked at me hard and said, "And you are?"

"Mary Steele, Mr. Tucker. You know my mom, I think?" I looked over my shoulder to where she stood and winced. When I'd touched Sarah, I'd revealed her to Mr. Tucker. Nothing good could come of this.

"Humph," Mr. Tucker said. "Junior, that the Jennings you was meeting?" He looked at Sarah, who stood a few feet behind me.

I saw a flash of panic pass across Mayor Tucker's face before he composed himself. "Well, yes sir. That is Sarah Jennings."

Mr. Tucker brushed past me, moving with surprising speed behind his walker, and headed toward Sarah. I froze. I didn't know if he would recognize the girl his daddy had killed, the girl he took a knife from to keep as a souvenir of his first lynching, . . . and if he did, I didn't know what would happen.

But fortunately, Mama was faster than I was and intercepted the old man. Her quick movement unstuck me, and I headed over just in time to hear her say, "Mr. Tucker, how nice to see you. I expect you know Beatrice from Channel 28?"

Surely, Mr. Tucker wouldn't make a scene with a reporter nearby. Surely.

The old man slowed just a bit and turned to look at his son. "You brought a reporter."

Mayor Tucker walked over beside Beatrice, and I saw her give him a quick nod.

"I did, Daddy. I thought it would make a great story for us to ask forgiveness of the Jennings family and share that publicly, be an example for the community. What do you think?"

The flush of crimson and the spittle at the corner of Mr. Tucker's thin, pale lips told me exactly what he thought. But what was he really going to say with a reporter there?

"Humph. Well, I suppose I should meet her."

Shamila had been standing with Sarah, an arm protectively over the girl's shoulder. I gave them a little wave, and the two walked over.

Sarah met my eye, and I gave her a nod.

"I'm Sarah Jennings, Mr. Tucker. We've met before."

The old man leaned back a bit, his hands still gripping his walker, and studied the young woman before him. "You do look a jot familiar."

"You was a little younger."

"Well, girl, I can't have been that much younger or else you wouldn't have been here."

I braced myself. Sarah looked at me, and I nodded. "Mr. Tucker, this is Bo Jennings's daughter. You met her on the night her mother was killed."

Mr. Tucker's brow furrowed, and then he leaned in close to me. "What's that you say, girl? I could have sworn you said this girl was that thief's daughter."

I saw the fury spread up Sarah's face, and I felt it flush mine.

But before either of us could say a thing, Mayor Tucker laid his hand gently on his father's back and said, "Daddy, you know Bo Jennings didn't steal anything, don't you?"

"No sir, I don't. My daddy said she was a thief, and I don't abide with no thieves."

"Daddy, Granddaddy lied. Ms. Jennings never took anything from the store."

"Boy, you better watch what you say about my father. He was a good man."

Mayor Tucker took a deep breath. "Yes, sir, I know he was in many ways, but not about this."

"I'm not going to stand here and listen to you sully your grandfather's good name." Mr. Tucker made his way back to his car, muttering under his breath.

I felt some of the tension dissipate as his car pulled away, but the anger lingered. I couldn't help, though, to also feel a bit of relief that Johnny Tucker hadn't made a big deal out of seeing a ghost. Maybe he hadn't realized that Sarah was dead? Or maybe he cared more about the fact that his family's secrets were getting out? Or maybe he was just racist enough for it not to matter to him at all?

"That bitter old man. He still believes the lies he was told when he was a kid," Sarah said.

I looked over at Mayor Tucker. He looked like he was going to cry. I didn't imagine it was easy to hear your father be so hateful.

Beatrice sat down on the bench. "Figures though. It's easier for most white folks to walk away than to deal with the truth, especially when the truth comes with a whole lot of shame and embarrassment, maybe even some guilt."

Mayor Tucker sat down next to Beatrice and put his head between his knees. Then, he lifted his face to Sarah and said, "What would you like me to do, Sarah? I can try to convince him about what really happened. I don't know if it'll work, but I can sure try."

Sarah sat down hard on the other side of the picnic table, her back to the mayor. "I appreciate the thought, Mr. Mayor, but I don't know that it would do a bit of good."

I couldn't disagree with her. I'd learned that people who were bound to hate were unlikely to untie themselves from it, and they were the only ones who could.

We all parted ways then, discouraged and disappointed but too tired to make plans, despite the mayor's goodwill. It only takes one racist to bring a whole community down, . . . but somehow I figured this wasn't going to be just about one hateful old man.

The next day after school, I went back to the historical society and asked Shamila if I could take another look at the files she'd pulled. I also asked if I could just spend time with them on my own. I didn't feel much like talking about things, not just now. But I did think maybe I could pull together enough information for an article in the local newspaper and a presentation at the memorial we had talked about. I had to do something productive, and I had to keep trying until I figured out what I needed to do to help Sarah free herself from that place. I knew we'd uncover the truth, knew we'd find a way to share it just like we had before, but right now, I had no idea what to do.

I spread out all the files on the big conference room table and began to go through them one by one: lots of letters, none with anything important, lots of handwritten family trees, again with nothing relevant, and newspaper articles recounting a very white-washed and completely inaccurate version of the story Sarah had told us the day before. I made notes on everything, putting together the most accurate account I could of Beverly Jennings's false arrest and subsequent lynching.

It was a tragic, horrible story. One that needed to be told truthfully. One that needed to be remembered, memorialized because Beverly Jennings's life mattered. I knew all this. I believed it.

Still, just telling the story didn't feel like enough. Maybe it never would. Maybe it never could.

I was just packing my notebook into my backpack and stacking the files when I noticed a slim file I had overlooked. It was simply labeled "Photos, 1928." I sat back down and took a deep breath, preparing to be horrified again by the photos of the lynching scene.

But when I opened the folder, I didn't see a lynching. I saw a couple—a black woman and a white man—sitting on the top of one of the walls of the boat lock, hand-in-hand. Their backs were to the camera so I couldn't tell who they were, but I knew this was scandalous for the time, long before the Loving case we'd studied in Mr. Meade's class ended miscegenation laws in Virginia. Black folks and white folks just didn't go together like that then, or if they did, they could get in big, big trouble for it.

I took a closer look at the photo, and then, just like in that art gallery in Lexington, the photo started to move. I could see the leaves on the trees shifting in a breeze I couldn't feel, and the water in the Maury River started to ripple. As I watched, the couple moved, too, turning to face each other, and I saw Sarah's profile clear as day.

She leaned in and kissed that boy.

After I texted Javier to come get me, I told Shamila I was leaving and borrowing a photo. She smiled and waved, knowing, I expect, that I wouldn't lose the picture and had good reason for wanting it.

I waited on the street and kept glancing at the picture, but there's only so much of watching your friend making out with someone that a girl can take. So eventually, I slid it between the pages of the copy of *Frankenstein* that I was reading when class got slow, and I began pacing back and forth.

I couldn't figure out why Sarah hadn't told me about this boy. I mean, I hadn't asked, "Were you dating a white boy?," but I figured this would have come up. Surely, Sarah must know this could have something to do with why her mom was killed.

I tried to imagine myself in Sarah's place, tried to imagine what it would feel like to have been the excuse people used to kill my mother. I couldn't imagine it, but I did realize Sarah might be feeling a good bit of shame and guilt herself. Seemed those were going around in droves these days.

As Javier drove me to the lock—I needed to talk with Sarah about the photo—I told him what I'd seen in the picture. He stared straight-ahead and stayed silent, but his jaw kept getting tighter and tighter the more I talked. I wasn't sure what was going on in his head. Javier got upset about these stories and the hatefulness like the rest of us did, but it didn't usually make him angry. And this was clearly Javier angry.

I stopped talking and looked at him. He glanced over at me and then pulled over to the shoulder. He kept his hands on the steering wheel and took a few deep breaths.

Finally, he said, "Mary, you realize people don't like the fact that we're dating, don't you?"

My face must have registered my surprise because Javier looked up at the ceiling of the car. "I love you, girl, but sometimes, you are so naïve."

I felt my face flush, and I wanted to cry. But I heard weight in

Javier's words and didn't want to make this about me if I could help it.

"Mary, my parents are immigrants from Mexico. They are here legally, but they aren't citizens. A lot of the people we know —or their parents at least—wish my parents and I would go back to 'where we came from.' " He made air quotes.

I opened my mouth to say I'd seen the news stories, but one thing I'd learned over the last few months was that it's usually better if I listen a whole lot more than I talk.

"My mother prays for me every day, prays that I won't get beat up by some person who thinks that not only are we taking their jobs but also their women."

I could taste bile in the back of my mouth. I am not anyone's woman.

"I don't think of you like that. You don't belong to me, of course." Javier took my hand. "But the people who think these things don't think much of women either. Mary, we could be Sarah and that boy."

I wanted to dismiss what he said, wanted to say "This is 2018. Things like this don't happen anymore." But I knew that wasn't true. I knew that our president wanted to create an America that was all white, that he was talking about revoking the citizenship of even people, like Javier, who were born here, that he was separating children from their parents and trying to raise money for a big wall to keep brown people like Javier out. I knew these things, but I hadn't really thought about how they affected me . . . or the people I loved.

I leaned over to Javier and put my hand on the side of his face. "You're right. I'm sorry. I should have thought about how this related to us, to you especially. White privilege strikes again."

He smiled. We talked about white privilege so much that it had almost become a phrase of endearment. Almost.

Then he kissed me, and for a second, I forgot everything else. Almost.

When we got to the boat lock, I saw Sarah. This time, she was sitting up on the lock wall just like she'd been in the picture. If I didn't know better, I'd think she knew that I knew.

She gave us a half-hearted wave as we got out of the car, and I felt my pulse quicken. I hated confrontation, and this felt like a confrontation. I climbed up the grass slope to the top of the lock and sat next to Sarah. Javier walked down by the river and began skipping stones. He hated confrontation even more than I did.

We sat for a while, just looking out over the river, and I marveled at the gentle way spring was painting the trees with a million different shades of green. Give it a couple of weeks, and the mountains would be a seamless sea of leaves. Now, they were simply shifting their weight forward into their fully-furled selves.

I took the picture of Sarah and the white boy out of my pocket and handed it to her.

She smiled. "Where did you get this?" Her voice was gentle, wistful even.

"It was in a folder at the historical society. That's you, isn't it?" I tried to keep the tone of accusation out of my voice, but I could still hear the edge.

"It is." Her voice was still quiet. "And that's Benjamin Tucker."

I jerked my head up. "Tucker?"

"That's right. That's Johnny Tucker's older brother. My boyfriend."

I felt anger rising in my throat. Why hadn't Sarah told me this to begin with? This changed everything. I felt betrayed, and I felt guilty for feeling betrayed.

Sarah interrupted my thoughts. "We was going to go north and get married soon as he graduated. We only had six months to go." Her voice broke, but she didn't cry. Instead, something about her seemed caved in, irrevocably broken.

I took a deep breath and let my anger out with it slowly. My

friend was hurting, and here I was about to lecture her for
keeping secrets, secrets she had needed to keep in order to stay
alive. Secrets that had killed her. "So that's why Guilford Tucker
accused your mom of stealing?"

"I suppose so. I didn't know nobody knew, but I guess this
picture proves somebody did. And somebody must have told
Benjamin's daddy." She kept on staring at the picture.

"So you didn't know? You didn't know that this is why . . ."

She glanced at me.

I sighed, but I still had questions. "This is awful, Sarah, but
how could you not know this is why they killed your mom?"

Sarah jerked her eyes to mine. "You think this is my fault?"
The sharpness of her voice could have cut me.

"Well, I mean—"

"Mary Steele. You're dating that brown boy down there, ain't
you? Would it be your fault if someone came and killed his
mama?"

I hadn't thought of it like that. "Well, no, of course not," I
sputtered. I wanted to get up and walk away, to put distance
between Sarah and me, between me and all this history, and that
was making today harder. I wanted it to be three days ago,
before I'd come here.

Sarah stared at me. She was angry, but beneath that frustration, I saw sadness in her eyes.

I took another deep breath and put my hand on my friend's
arm and said, "I'm sorry."

Sarah just nodded and looked back at the picture. "Besides,
could have been anything that they went after my mama for.
They didn't really need no excuse."

I remembered Emmett Till and shivered.

Then, Sarah squinted at the picture and then looked up at
me. "How you know this was me anyway?"

I blew a hard puff of air out of my mouth and explained this
part of this thing I could do, the part that made certain
photographs move.

Sarah shook her head and rolled her eyes up, but then she smiled. "You strange, Mary. You know that, right?"

I laughed. "I do. Glad you know it too."

She laughed, and then we were both laughing so hard we had to hold our bellies. Our voices bounced off the stones of the lock below.

"Anything else you can do like this?" she asked when she caught her breath.

I looked down at the picture in her hands and then met her eyes. "Not that I know of," I said. "I hope not."

11

*T*hat night, with Sarah's permission, I caught everyone up on her relationship with Benjamin Tucker and the photograph of them at the lock. Isaiah thought we should go straight to the mayor with this new information, see what he might make of it, and Javier agreed, but the rest of us didn't think that would do much good. After all, we knew who had killed Ms. Jennings and Sarah. Now, we knew the motive, but even that we'd already kind of known: racism, just now a specific shade of it.

As we hashed this all out via text message, I kept thinking about the statute of limitations on murder, about how if these men were still alive they could be tried for their crimes, about how Johnny Tucker could probably be charged with being an accessory. There was a tiny part of me—a sharp, angry part—that wanted to go after the racist old man, make him pay for his attitudes, for not trying to know better. But most of me knew that taking an old man to trial—an old man who was a staple of our community—would only bring grief to good people and probably no justice to him at all. That tiny sharp part was hard to silence though.

Over the next few days, we continued to gather information

about Beverly Jenning's lynching, and Shamila reached out to the Equal Justice Initiative about having her added to the memorial wall. The task required a little documentation but nothing copious since, of course, most lynchings were quiet affairs, at least officially, even if dozens of white people showed up to watch.

Mr. Meade did his usual and turned the memorial to Ms. Jennings into an extra credit class project, and most of our classmates signed up to help. We made flyers and wrote articles for the school paper and Charlottesville's *Daily Progress*. We contacted local news stations and arranged for a Baptist preacher to be there too since Sarah and her mother were Baptists. We talked with Sarah about what her mother liked: Gospel music, a good banana pudding, and rocking on the front porch in the evening were her favorites. So we arranged a gospel choir from the Virginia Military Institute to be at the memorial service, and we held a banana pudding competition, with Mayor Tucker and Isaiah as the judges, to raise money for a trip to Mississippi to deliver the earth to the Equal Justice Initiative Memorial. Mom arranged for the local Cracker Barrel to donate two rocking chairs to sit on the porch at the historical society in Beverly Jennings's honor.

We were good at these things, good at events and remembering. Good at the public part of healing. And I was glad for all we were doing, but it felt like we were falling short, not doing enough. While each of the public events held to address racial injustice is necessary, there are only so many you can do before you feel like you're just *performing* the work of healing. At least I felt like I was performing. There had to be more.

On the Friday night the week after I first saw Sarah, Mom and I sat down to watch the all-female *Ghostbusters*. She was aching for a little bit of a throw-back, and I just needed something at least a little funny to lift my mood. Plus, the irony of me watching a movie about going after ghosts was not lost on me. Over the past year and a half, my friends had bought me Ghost

Hunters T-shirts, full sets of the *Ghost Adventures* DVDs, and a wide array of figurines and stuffed animals of Stay Puft, the giant marshmallow man from *Ghostbusters*. They thought they were funny, . . . and I did too.

Mom and I had just gotten the DVD to actually play— Redbox discs weren't always awesome—when the doorbell rang. We live in a town where people are neighborly out and about, but people don't usually just show up at one another's houses without calling first. So an unexpected guest was a rarity . . . and not necessarily a welcome one tonight.

Mom opened the door, and there stood Mayor Tucker. He didn't look well. In fact, he looked downright ashen.

"Mayor Tucker, you okay? Come in. Sit down. I'll get you some tea." Mom's universal fix for everything was hot tea, and it usually did the trick.

The mayor collapsed onto the sofa and folded his hands behind his head before letting out a long sigh. Then, he noticed the TV. "Oh, Mary, I'm sorry. Ya'll were about to watch something, and I interrupted. I should have called."

"No, sir. It's fine. You okay?" I pushed the power button on the TV and then turned toward him, my legs crossed in front of me on the couch.

He let out another long sigh. "Frankly, Mary. I'm not. I got some hard news, and I came over as soon as I heard. I knew you needed to know."

I tried to keep my face neutral, but if I said I wasn't expecting some hard news in all this, I would be lying. "Well, thanks for coming."

Mom came back in with the tea and handed it to the mayor before taking a seat on the brick hearth by the fireplace.

"Daddy has mustered up his buddies, and he's planning to protest your memorial. Claims we don't need to be remembering a woman who was a thief."

"Seriously?" Mom's voice was full of contained anger. "The man is going to protest the memorial service to a woman who was murdered, who was murdered by his father? Has he no shame?"

I agreed with Mom, of course, but I saw the mayor wince at her harsh words. This was still his father, and even if he saw the man in his full regalia of hatred, it was a sure bet he still carried some positive memories of trips for ice cream or tossing a football around the yard. "Mayor Tucker, why do you think your daddy is doing this?"

"Pride, Mary. He feels like he needs to uphold his daddy's good name." The mayor let out another long sigh. "As if *his* reputation is more important than the truth, more important than honoring a woman's life. Besides, no matter what Beverly Jennings did—if anything—she didn't deserve to be lynched, stealing flour or not."

It was my turn to sigh now. "She didn't steal flour or anything else, Mayor. I know why your grandfather and those men killed her."

The mayor sat forward and turned toward me. "You do?"

I got up and took the picture out of my backpack. I had tried to leave it with Sarah, but she pointed out that she didn't have pockets to store such a thing in, and she wanted it taken care of. I kept it in my bag since I wanted to have it with me if she ever wanted to see it, and my backpack went with me everywhere.

Before I handed it to the mayor, I explained that I could see people moving in old photos sometimes, and so I had been able to see that this was Sarah Jennings when I found it. I never would get used to telling people about these things I could do.

He looked a bit puzzled, but only for a second. Once you had seen and talked with a ghost because a teenage girl could see them, I guess it wasn't a hard jump, then, to think she could also see people move in photos.

He looked from the photo to me and back to the photo over and over again. "She confirmed it," I said.

"And the boy . . ."

I swallowed hard. "It's your uncle, Benjamin."

The mayor leaned back on the couch and stared at the photo. "Uncle Ben? This keeps getting worse. Well, maybe not worse. Worse than a lynching doesn't really exist. But worse for my family."

I gave Mom a look.

The mayor must have seen me because he said, quickly, "Oh, not that it's worse because Uncle Ben and Sarah were dating. . . . No, nothing like that. Just that our family's ugliness is getting more and more ugly all the time." He reached over to hand the photo to me, and for a moment, both of us were touching it.

"Whoa!" He jerked upright on the couch and dropped the photo. "They moved."

Sarah and Benjamin had been moving the whole time for me, so it took me a second to register what he meant. . . . He saw them move.

I picked the photo up from the couch cushion and looked at it again, and then, I took the mayor's hand and placed the photo in it while I kept two fingers gripping the corner. I saw his eyes go wide. "You can see them kissing?"

"I can." His voice was soft and breathless, awed. "I can."

We sat for a few moments, watching Sarah and Benjamin, but when we both began to shift in our seats because of the awkwardness of watching two people make out, I let go of the photo. The mayor set it on the coffee table in front of him.

Mayor Tucker rubbed the palms of his hands into his eyes and said, "Mary Steele, girl, is there anything else you can do?"

"Sarah asked me the same thing yesterday." I gave a breathy chuckle because the more people asked me this, the more I worried that I might not know all I could do yet. That prospect did not sit well with me. "Not that I know of, but until a few minutes ago, I didn't know that I could let other people see photos move, so who knows?" My voice sounded light, like I was joking, but what I felt was a knot of concern in my belly.

Mom had been sitting quietly by the fire, but now, she got up and came to sit on the arm of the couch next to me. She placed her arm around my shoulders and pulled me close. I felt myself relax just a bit.

"So Mayor Tucker, what do we do now?" Mom said.

The mayor let out a slow exhale. "Well, I need to confront my father head-on. Get him to stop this ridiculous protest against the memorial."

Mom nodded. "Need help with that? I could go with—"

"Thank you, Ms. Steele," Mayor Tucker interrupted to say, "but I think I best handle this on my own. Don't need to subject anyone else to the ugliness. I appreciate the offer though."

"We have the memorial set for next Friday, Good Friday," Mom said. "Seemed a fitting day to remember Ms. Jennings. The program's all set, but we'd love for you to give the welcome if you would, Mr. Mayor."

Mom's request must have pulled the mayor out of a reverie because he shook his head a bit before saying, "Oh, of course. I'd be honored." Then he stood up. "I best be going. Like I said, I just wanted you all to know what was happening." He headed for the door. "But you one-upped me on news tonight."

"Sorry about that—"

"Don't apologize, Mary. It's always better to know the truth. Always."

After Mayor Tucker left, Mom and I started our movie, but most of it didn't even register. I was too busy imagining what the mayor was going to say to his father . . . and if he was going to mention me.

The weekend was uneventful except for my fretting over what might happen with Johnny Tucker if he really paid attention to the fact that he'd met a ghost and that I was the reason he could see her. Good ole boys don't often have a soft spot for people who can do magical things, no matter how much they talk about Jesus and his miracles.

I thought about going to see Sarah, but I just couldn't muster the energy. I didn't know what to say, and worse, I still didn't understand why I could see her. She didn't know that there was a reason for me to meet each of the ghosts I saw, there was something only I could do to bring their peace. I'd learned that much in my experiences. But I knew, . . . and I needed time to think and figure that out. It couldn't be about finding the people who killed her mother and her. We'd already done that. Maybe it was about the memorial, a public remembrance of their story. But somehow, I doubted that was it either. That didn't feel weighty enough, crucial enough. I was making myself anxious with all my puzzling over it.

I tried to keep busy by hanging flyers and talking to people about the memorial on Friday, but by the time Monday morning rolled around, I was a wreck. I hadn't slept much, and I had eaten far too many chocolate chip cookies from the batch Mom and I made on Sunday afternoon. I was edgy and testy, and when Javier picked me up for school, the last thing I felt like doing was talking.

"Morning," I said as I dropped into the front seat of his car.

"Well, aren't you just a bundle of joy?"

My eyes cut to him and then stared silently out the windshield. A lesser man would have just let me sulk, but Javier knew me, and he knew that the only way out of my funk was for me to talk it out. But he also knew that saying that would not bode well for him.

"So I was thinking . . . Sarah mentioned that she had a brother, right? Jacob? Jonathan?"

"Joshua. His name was Joshua." I knew Javier knew that. I could see what he was doing, but I couldn't resist. "But he'd be dead by now." I cringed at the bite in my voice.

"Of course he would be, but what if he had kids? They might be alive? And they might have kids?"

I had to give it to him. I was feeling better already. Here, here, was the answer to why I could see Sarah. Maybe. "That's true. So how do we find that out?" But of course, I knew the answer.

We went straight to Mr. Meade's classroom and got a pass to miss homeroom to do research in the computer lab. Within minutes, we had entered what we knew about Joshua Jennings: name, place of residence, born about 1914 based on the fact that he was fourteen at the time of the lynching, . . . and there they were. His wife was named Delia, and his daughters were Josephine and Anne. Anne had died in 2010, but it looked like Josephine might still be alive.

A few more minutes of research showed that at the time of the last census, Josephine was here in Terra Linda. Eight years is a long time, so it was possible she'd moved, but I figured if she'd been living here for more than seventy years, it was worth a shot to see if she were still here. I learned she'd gotten married in 1952 to a man named Dick Garrison, so I checked the online white pages and found her there, right on Fifth Street— Josephine Garrison.

It took all the will power I had to not leave the building right then and walk the few blocks to Mrs. Garrison's house, but I knew that, first of all, I'd get in big trouble, and second of all, I needed to think a bit before I told a woman that I knew her aunt who had died ninety years earlier.

At lunch that day, Nicole, Marcie, Javier and I made a plan about how to talk with Mrs. Garrison about the death of her great-aunt and aunt. I was adamant that we could not tell her I could see ghosts. When they tried to assure me that it was no big deal, I insisted. They seemed a little put-out, but then, they weren't the ones who randomly appeared places and carried the responsibility of bringing the soul of another human being to peace after decades of turmoil. So they wisely didn't push it.

We decided we would tell her we were doing a project for history class about lynchings, which was true and also a story we'd used before to good success. Since her family's story was public—at least in the strictest sense since it was in the newspaper—we figured this was plausible, and we hoped she might be eager to share the story. I would call her after school and set up a time for us all to get together.

As soon as I got to Javier's car that afternoon, I dialed Mrs.

Garrison's number. She picked up on the third ring. "Hello, Mrs. Garrison. My name is Mary Steele, and I'm calling—"

"I know why you're calling. Sarah told me, and I want no part of it."

I sat there silently for several moments. She'd said *Sarah*, but she couldn't mean my Sarah, could she?

"Ms. Steele, are you still there?"

"Um, yes, ma'am. I'm sorry. I think I misheard you. Did you say that Sarah told you who I was?"

"Yes, you heard me correctly. My aunt Sarah told me that you knew what had happened to her and her mother, and I'm glad she finally has someone her age to talk to, but I will have no part in remembering that awful day."

I realized, somewhere in my mind, that I was feeling disappointed about Mrs. Garrison's lack of interest in our memorial, but I couldn't bring that emotion to the surface because of the hard, thick skin of shock that had settled over me.

I managed to say, "I understand. Do you mind me asking you a question about Sarah, though? Just between the two of us."

I heard her sigh, but then she said, "Alright, dear. What do you want to know?"

"How long have you been able to see Sarah, Mrs. Garrison?"

"Well, from the time I was your age, dear. That's when these things usually manifest." She paused. "I wish you well, Ms. Steele, but if that is all . . ."

My Southern politeness kicked in, and even though it was far from "all" and I could have tumbled over myself with questions, I said, "Yes, ma'am. Thank you for your time." And I hung up the phone.

12

_I_ sat there on the hood of Javier's car for a long time and watched the parking lot empty. Javier eventually made his way down to the lot after meeting with his bandmates about the benefit concert they were having for the EJI trip, but I hardly noticed when he sat down beside me. _Someone else could see ghosts._ I didn't know how to begin to make sense of that, but the person who could understand what I was going through wasn't interested in talking with me.

Eventually, I roused myself enough to tell Javier about the call—poor guy had just been sitting there waiting and playing Candy Crush.

"So she drops this bomb on you and then doesn't want to talk about it or about Sarah either." Javier shook his head. "The nerve of some people."

I knew that I should probably agree with Javier, especially given how frustrated I was feeling, but instead, I found myself defending Mrs. Garrison. "You don't know how it is, Javier. To be able to do this thing." I was almost shouting. "You can't know how hard this is." I stood up and started to walk away.

"Hey, hey. Okay. Sorry. I'm on your side." His voice was soft and more than a little bit wounded as he walked over to me.

"You're right. I *don't* know. But I still think the kind thing would have been for her to help you understand."

Then, the tears came. I knew they would. They always did when I was upset, and these came from a place way down that held all the loneliness of this ability. I sat down on a concrete parking stop and let go. I let all the worry, all the weight, all the responsibility wash down my face. I must have cried for ten minutes, and when I finished, it wasn't because I felt better. It was because I'd come to a decision.

"Get in," I told Javier.

He climbed into the driver's seat. "Where to?"

"Fifth Street."

He started the car, and I was off to get some answers.

When we pulled up in front of Mrs. Garrison's house, I gave Javier a kiss on the cheek and stepped out. "Text everyone okay?"

He smiled, and I walked up and rang the bell. I saw the curtains beside the window move over and then back, and then the door opened.

"I figured you'd be by." Mrs. Garrison was a tiny woman, not even five feet tall, but she stood as straight as a rod and looked like she could take down a bear on her own. Her gray hair was pulled back in a tight bun that reminded me of what Bo Jennings had worn, and she had on a tidy outfit of blue pants and a coordinated floral shirt. Even her earrings were the same shade of blue. She looked the picture of a Southern woman, but her wide-legged stance in the center of the doorway didn't speak of that quintessential Southern hospitality that would invite me in for sweet tea.

"I need to know more, Mrs. Garrison. I understand you don't want to talk about it, but I need to talk about it. You can understand that, right?"

She didn't budge and kept her gaze straight up into my eyes. I took a small step back; I didn't want to tower over the woman. I wasn't here to intimidate. Mine was more of a begging mission.

So I told her all that had happened with Moses and Charlotte and the twelve children. I told her about my family and about how I'd come to see Sarah. I told her about the mayor. I told her everything, and when I was done, she gave me one last, long stare, and then she stepped aside and motioned me in.

Her house looked like most of the others in downtown Terra Linda. A front living room spanned most of the left side of the house, and a hallway turned to the right to what, I assumed, were the bedrooms and bathroom. Mrs. Garrison motioned to her stylish gray sofa and took a seat in a wing chair across the room.

"Mary Steele. I've heard a lot about you."

"From the ghosts?" As soon as the words left my mouth, I felt foolish.

"No, girl. From the newspaper." Mrs. Garrison cracked a small smile. "'From the ghosts?' What do you think this is? One of those ghost-hunting TV shows?"

I felt my face flush, but a small smile crept to the corners of my mouth. "No, ma'am."

"You and your squad been doing a lot of work these past few months."

"Yes, ma'am." My smile got even bigger. Hearing an old woman use the word *squad* cracked me up.

"I've been following. Didn't know for sure that you had the ghost thing until I talked with Sarah the other night, though."

I nodded, not sure if I was allowed to ask questions, yet.

"She likes you," Mrs. Garrison said. "Sarah doesn't like much of anybody, but she likes you. That's ninety percent of why I let you in my house."

"What's the other 10 percent?"

"Spunk. I appreciate a woman with spunk."

I didn't even try to suppress my grin this time, and she gave me a sideways smile too. "Alright, Ms. Steele, what do you want to know?"

The excitement about the opportunity to talk about all this

with someone else who had experienced it welled up in me and made it impossible for my mind to land on a question. I sat there with my mouth hanging open.

"Okay then. Maybe it would help for you to hear about the first time I saw a ghost?"

"Yes, ma'am."

Mrs. Garrison settled back in her chair and nested her hands in her lap. "I was 16, I think. Walking home from school. Then, *poof!* I was standing beside a stream up on Larch Lane. You know it?"

I nodded. It ran right up near my house.

"There in front of me was a little boy. Maybe six, seven years old. He had a fishing line in the water, and he was just staring straight ahead. I was so befuddled by what had just happened to me that I must have stood there for several minutes before I thought to speak. But when I did, that little boy just about climbed out of his britches."

"Well, it didn't take long for me to figure out—probably same as you—that this little boy was dead. You know they have that kind of transparent look to them."

I nodded vehemently.

"This little boy had been dead about eighty years. Been killed by a little white boy who wanted that fishing rod he was holding. I was the first person he'd talked to since he died."

I swallowed hard.

"Every day I could, I went back to that stream and talked to little Homer. Tried to keep him company. Until finally one day, an old white man came up on the stream when I was there. He sure was surprised to find a black girl sitting there by his stream. And I was terrified—there, all alone with a white man."

I could picture it. I'd even lived my version of it. I felt nervous for that girl, even here in her living room more than seventy years later. I leaned forward in my seat.

"Homer told me that was the boy who killed him. That this old man came by once in a while, never said anything, just stood there by the stream and watched the river. Homer had tried to talk to him, to tell him it was okay, that he knew the man was sorry, but of course, the man couldn't hear him."

I found myself leaning forward in my seat like I was waiting for the climax of some TV drama.

"I'll never forget it. Homer said, very quietly, 'Would you tell him I forgive him?' I must have moved my head really fast to look at Homer because the white man took a step back. I expect he thought I was a little unwell in the head. But I stood and gently said, "Sir, Homer wants you to know he forgives you.'"

Mrs. Garrison laughed and drew her hands high up over her head. "It was so ingrained in me to think it was the black person's job to do the fixing that I thought for sure Homer would have peace now, that he'd move on. But he didn't. I could still see him clear as day."

I nodded again. I knew what she meant. Sometimes, I'd felt like that, too, that when someone had done wrong by me, I had to do all the work to make it right.

"That man looked at me. He didn't seem surprised to hear Homer's name or that I had a message from him. He just looked sad. He sat down beside me in his fine clothes and said, 'That day, my mama told me to go get that colored boy out of our stream, that he was dirtying it up. I didn't want to. Didn't see the harm in that boy fishing, but my mama was fearsome. So up I went. I didn't mean to kill him though, just wanted to scare him off.'"

Mrs. Garrison's voice had gotten very quiet, and she was looking at the fireplace across the room. "Then, he said something I had never heard a white person say before. 'Please tell him I'm sorry.' It felt like the whole world tilted for me then, so strong were those words."

"It took me a minute to gather myself, but when I did, Homer had gone. I don't know if it was the apology, the truth coming out into the air, or what, but he'd moved along."

I sat back in my seat and let a long push of air stream out of my nose.

"That was my first time. I don't know that I could count how many times there have been since. seventy years worth of ghosts."

I didn't even begin to know how to process the idea of seeing ghosts for the next seventy years . . . for the rest of my life, and deep down, I didn't want to. It wasn't something I looked forward to.

My face must have shown what I was thinking because Mrs. Garrison said, "It gets easier. Not easy, mind you, but easier. You start to know what you can do and what you can't." Her face took on a soft expression, and she got up from her chair and came over to sit beside me. "Child, you've been doing a lot for these people. I've seen you working hard, watched you on the news and in the newspaper. You didn't start out with easy ones, that's for sure. But you're doing well. Hear me, though, you can't go this hard your whole life. Sometimes, you're going to just have to let them be while things come to pass. You hear what I'm saying?"

Inside me, I felt something shift, a little light shining. With that light came a release, and I was embarrassed to feel myself begin to cry. This woman had been hesitant to even talk to me, and here I was crying. "Thank you for your time, Mrs. Garrison. I hear you. I'll think about what you said."

I tried to stand up, but Mrs. Garrison put her hand on my knee. "Mary, do you know why I didn't want to talk to you on the phone?"

I wiped the tears from under my eyes and shook my head.

"Because I needed to know you took what we can do seriously. I needed to see you really want to understand, so I shut you down. Maybe that wasn't the right way to go about it—this is my first time meeting someone else who can see ghosts, too— but I needed to know you understood that what we do is important."

I looked up at her, and she was watching me with a gentle smile. "I am serious, Mrs. Garrison. This is hard, and I don't really know what I'm doing and—" I felt the tears returning so I stopped talking.

Mrs. Garrison reached over and pulled me close to her side. "Well, at least we don't have to do this alone anymore." She didn't say this in that bright, shiny voice people sometimes use to try and pretend that things are better. Rather, her voice was gentle and a bit sad. I leaned into her.

We sat for a few minutes that way, just quietly, before she stirred. "So, Mary Steele, what are we going to do about our friend Sarah?"

I cleared my throat and said, "I think you should see something." I took the picture of Sarah and Benjamin out of my pocket and placed it on the coffee table. "Did you know about Benjamin?"

She picked the photo up, and I saw a flash of something, maybe fear, pass across her face. "Where did you get this photo?"

"The historical society. You've never seen it?"

She handed it back to me. "No, never. But that does change things a bit."

"What do you mean?"

"Well," she stood up and walked to the other side of the room, "I knew about Benjamin. Sarah had told me about him years ago. But I didn't know that anyone else knew, particularly anybody else from then." She paced back and forth in front of me. "This means, well, you know what this means."

"It means that they killed Sarah's mother because she was dating Benjamin Tucker."

"Yes." She let out a long sigh. "Benjamin Tucker was my grandfather."

She was looking out the window when she spoke, so I thought I must have misheard her. "Excuse me? I'm sorry, but I thought I heard you say that Benjamin Tucker was your grandfather. But Sarah is your aunt, right?"

Mrs. Garrison sat down. "That's what Grandmama Bo wanted everyone to think. She knew how much danger Sarah would be in if anyone found out she and Ben had had a child. So she gently led everyone to think I was Uncle Josh's child and that the mother had run off. Easy enough to convince most folks, especially white folks, that a young black girl wouldn't take responsibility for her choices."

I winced.

"But of course, Sarah took good care me. Sarah raised a garden to help feed me and make me a doll before I was even born. That's what Uncle Josh told me when I was old enough. He was the one who, ironically, ended up raising me after . . ." She let her voice trail off.

Sarah had raced down to stop the men who were going to lynch her mother not just because she knew they were going after Bo because of her relationship with Benjamin but because her mother had been protecting her all along.

"So Bo knew?"

"She knew. And she didn't care. Uncle Josh always said that Grandmama liked Ben, treated him like a son. She wished they hadn't gotten pregnant so young, but she knew kids would be kids." Mrs. Garrison paused and let out a long slow breath. "She was protecting Ben too. Lord knows what would have happened to him if his family . . . well, I guess they did find out."

I looked down at the picture on the sofa between us. Someone had found out and had told the Tuckers, and they had made a statement without ever having to make public the fact that Ben had a black daughter. "Lord, have mercy." I tried to say it like I'd heard tough, old women say it—with fervor and fight —but it came out as a prayer, which was just as well. "What happened to Ben?"

"They sent him away to a military school over in the center of the state. Paid a lot of money to keep him away. He'd come by and see me when he could—at holidays and such—but eventually, Uncle Josh told him it was probably for the best if he just didn't come again."

"What?! Didn't they think you would want to know your Daddy?"

She snapped her eyes at me. "Of course they did. But there are worse things than not knowing your father, Mary Steele. Far worse things."

I knew that was true. Knew it well, but I was still angry on Mrs. Garrison's behalf. She should have had a say.

"Years later, we reconnected. He'd always stayed in touch; he'd sent letters and presents for birthdays, but it took fifteen years for me to see him again. I'd missed my daddy. But my uncle did the best thing he knew to do. And because of it, I got to know my daddy a lot longer than I didn't know him. That may not have been true if he'd kept coming around." Mrs. Garrison looked me hard in the face. "We didn't need another lynching, and I was only a baby girl, Mary."

I nodded. To imagine that people would kill a toddler was almost impossible, but I knew that almost impossible and impossible were two very different things. And if they were willing to shoot a teenage girl for trying to save her own mother
. . .

"I'm going to make myself a cup of peppermint tea. Would you like some?" Mrs. Garrison was now standing over me with a gentle smile on her face.

"Yes, please. Can I help?"

She smiled, and we walked into the kitchen. It was a long, narrow room, and each side was covered in white cabinets. The countertop looked new—a black stone with silver flecks in it—and a bright-red mixer stood in one corner next to a plate of what had to be homemade cookies.

"Want one?" Mrs. Garrison followed my line of vision and took the plastic wrap off the plate.

"Thank you." I picked up a cookie and took a small bite.

Then a bigger one. "This is delicious," I said with my mouth full, forgetting all my manners.

"Thank you. Grandmama Bo's recipe." She leaned closer and whispered. "The secret is the cream of tartar."

I had no idea what cream of tartar was, but if it made cookies taste like this, I was going to get some and sprinkle it on everything.

Mrs. Garrison poured three mugs of tea and sent me to get Javier from his car. Then, we spent another hour or so telling her about school and what we were doing with the lynching memorial, and she told us about her years as a school teacher. She said she'd known my mom but hadn't ever taught her. She'd taught Isaiah though, and I couldn't wait to tell him I knew the tale of the lunch box stomping. (Apparently, little Isaiah had quite the temper.)

Eventually, the sun started to drop close to the top of the mountains, and we knew it was time for us to go. I had one last question before we left. "Mrs. Garrison, would you be interested in coming to the memorial service we are having for your grandmother? I mean, I know you're not really interested—"

She interrupted me. "Mary, I thought you'd never ask."

I gave her a puzzled look. "My hesitation earlier was not about remembering my grandmother. It was about sharing my secrets. But now that I know you—and you, Javier—I know my secrets are safe with you. I'll be there, and I'd be happy to say a few words if you'd like, as Sarah's niece, of course."

"We'd love that. Thank you." I meant it, even if I felt uneasy with having her do such a public thing with so many private stories behind it. "Can I give you a hug?"

"Of course."

I put my arms around her shoulders and hugged her gently, and she squeezed me back so tight I thought my ribs would break.

13

*T*he next day after school, I had a good conversation with Sarah about her daughter. "Glad you know now. Sorry I couldn't tell you."

I shook my head. "No worries. But can I ask you something?" She looked me straight on, and I took that as a yes.

"Tell me about Benjamin?" I asked her as we sat by the river on that sunny afternoon. "I mean, was he cute?"

Her eyes cut to me like she was annoyed. "He was alright," she said as a huge grin broke across her face. "He was the most beautiful boy in the world, and he treated me good. Brought me flowers. Walked me home. Opened the car door for me." A shadow crossed her face. "When we were able to ride in the front seat together. Most times I had to lie down in the back seat until we got to my neighborhood."

I couldn't even imagine having to hide because you weren't allowed to ride in the car with a white boy. Or rather, that white boy wasn't allowed to ride with you.

"But it was good. Really good." She looked down at her legs. "Too good sometimes."

I sat still and waited. If she was going to tell me about

Josephine, I wanted it to be because she trusted me, not because I made her feel like she had to.

"She was a good baby. Laughed at everything. Didn't cry much, not even when she fell down." Sarah smiled. "She had the fattest thighs, like two big pork loins, and they were ticklish too." She sat there smiling until a tear dropped off the tip of her nose.

"You miss her." I wasn't asking a question, just clearing a space in case Sarah wanted to say so. I knew she could still see her daughter, but I also knew that seeing her wasn't the same as raising her.

"Sometimes, it hurts so bad that I feel like my chest is cracking open. If I had knowed . . ."

But she didn't need to finish the statement. If she had known a lot of things, then things would have turned out different. But what do any of us know about the way our story will go?

That question would come to haunt me over the next few days.

The planning for Friday's service was moving right along. A food truck from Lexington was coming over to serve hot donuts and apple cider. The gospel choir was all set. The mayor had prepared a speech, and Mrs. Garrison was ready for her part as well. Sarah had even asked me to bring her a brush so she could fix her hair before the big day.

Not that we planned on having Sarah make an appearance to anyone but those of us who could see her already. Neither of us wanted to become the focus of the attention. But she did want to look her best for her mother's service.

On Thursday evening, we all gathered at our house to go over the plans one last time. Mom had gotten all the ingredients for a homemade pizza bar, and I was there for some pepperoni and mushroom goodness. Nicole and Javier had just gotten their pizzas out of the oven, and we were all gathered around the fireplace, eating and talking and laughing when Stephen came in. He'd just gotten off his shift and was joining us a bit late to update us on what the Terra Linda police department would be doing tomorrow. It made me a little sad to know we needed police officers on hand, but we'd learned the hard way that they were necessary for events since people determined to stand strong in their hate often showed up to make a scene. Stephen grabbed a soda from the kitchen and sat down on the couch.

"Make yourself a pizza, Stephen," Mom urged.

"Thank you, Ms. Steele. I will, but I thought ya'll would want to hear about this right away."

I felt my stomach sink.

We must have all looked pretty wary, because Stephen said quickly, "No, no. It's good news. *Good Morning America* is coming to cover the memorial service tomorrow. They'll run the story on Monday."

The energy in the room picked up, and suddenly everyone was talking at once. I wanted to be excited with them, but this news left me breathless with dread. I couldn't help worrying that someone might find out about what I could do, and then, my life as I knew it would be over. I had flashes of needing to go into a make-shift witness protection program just to get a night's sleep.

But everyone else was so thrilled about Stephen's announcement that I tried to seem just as excited. Once everyone settled a bit, Isaiah asked, "How did this happen?"

"Well apparently, the local ABC affiliate got the press release that Beatrice created," he looked at the reporter, who was just taking a bite of an artichoke and sausage slice, "and they passed it up to ABC national. The department only found out about their visit this afternoon because they wanted to be sure there was some sort of security since they had heard some protestors were going to be on site."

The room grew very quiet, and Stephen looked puzzled. "Oh, don't worry about that. It's just a bunch of local guys: Johnny Tucker and his friends. Old guys. We'll watch them, but really, there's no reason to worry."

I squinted at him. "You know that Johnny Tucker was there that day, that his father killed Bo?"

He came over and sat next to me on the hearth. "I do, but I also know he's a lot of bluster and no fight. He's got a big mouth and an ugly attitude, but he really is harmless."

Stephen's assurances seemed to calm everyone else's nerves, but I had a bad feeling, . . . and unfortunately, my feelings were almost always right.

Friday after school, Javier, Marcie, Nicole, and I headed to the lock. We had all tried to convince our parents to let us go early and miss the last two periods of the day, which were always a joke on Fridays anyway. But all of them said no. Mom specifically said, "There is nothing happening at the lock that can't wait two hours."

For once, though, Mom was wrong. By the time we got there, all of Route 60 was lined with cars, and the state troopers were out directing traffic. We had to park way down past the Coffee Pot and then walk back up the highway. I was not happy.

The entire meadow around the lock was full of people. News crews were set up by the river and on top of the boulders nearby. I could even see a cameraman on the bluff across the Maury, and I thought I heard a drone overhead. It didn't take long to spot the Good Morning America crew because a huge crowd was gathered around Michael Strahan as he signed autographs at the picnic tables. Robin Roberts was nearby, too, but I guess an eloquent woman still doesn't garner as much interest as a former pro athlete.

Mom waved us over to the sycamore, where she and Sarah were standing with Shamila and Isaiah. Sarah and I had agreed to stay a good distance apart lest I bump into her and show her to the world, so I stood on the other side of Mom and just gave her a little wave. Nothing big though. Didn't want to draw attention that way either.

"Glory day," Shamila said. "I haven't seen a crowd this big

since that woman from the Trump administration was kicked out of the Red Hen restaurant."

That had been the day Lexington became famous, and the fame wasn't all pleasant, even though most of us quietly rooted that restaurant owner on.

I could see the gospel choir over on their risers, and Mayor Tucker and Mrs. Garrison were by the stage we'd borrowed from the high school. It looked like everyone was here, and we were about fifteen minutes from starting when a charter bus stopped on 60.

At first, we thought they were just folks here because they were interested in attending the memorial. Shamila said that ceremonies like this sometimes drew large crowds, that sometimes local retirement homes would bring folks as an outing. But when we saw the third Confederate flag come out the door, we knew this wasn't a bunch of retirees looking for an afternoon's activity. We were in for something horrible.

I scanned the crowd for Stephen and saw him over by the GMA tent. I sprinted that way, and he saw me coming. I waved toward the bus, and he was on his radio quicker than I could reach him.

"Need more officers immediately" was all I heard him say.

I was sad to say that bad feeling had been right.

"What in the world?" Stephen said as we walked toward the bus. "You better wait here, Mary." I didn't want him going over there alone, but I saw Mr. Meade catch up to him, and I let out the breath I'd been holding.

Javier came over and walked me away toward the stage. "You okay?"

I didn't even begin to know how to answer that, but I had opened my mouth to say yes when I noticed that a bunch of the men—all white men—were pointing at me and headed this way.

"Uh oh." It wasn't my most articulate statement of dread, but it said what I needed to convey.

The men were almost to me when Stephen sprinted between us and said, "Mary, go over by Michael Strahan. Now. Fast."

I knew what he wanted—cameras—and I took off at a dead run, Javier right behind me. I slid in next to Strahan like I'd known him all my life, and he took it in stride, dropping a giant hand on my shoulder. But I could feel him tense when he saw the crowd with the flags headed his way. He signaled to the camerawoman nearby, and she started rolling. He picked up his mic and said, without a moment's hesitation, "We're so happy to be live here in Lexington, Virginia, for the memorial that will commemorate the life and remember the violent death by lynching of Beverly Jennings."

The angry white men slowed their pace when they saw the camera, and after a quick exchange of words, they detoured away a bit. But I couldn't let myself relax yet. I gave Strahan a big smile and slid out from under his arm and toward my mom, Javier's arm around my waist.

I was almost in tears when I reached her. "They recognized me, Mom. They pointed at me." My breathing was shallow, and I felt faint.

"Sit down, Mary. Head between your knees."

I did what she said and took advantage of the chance to catch my breath and hide for a minute.

"What happened?" She had been focused on getting everything arranged on the stage, so I guess she'd missed the arrival of the bus.

I saw Stephen moving fast through the crowd as the other police officers moved toward the bus. "A group of white nationalists just got off that bus. Johnny Tucker called them. They're part of the same group that was in Charlottesville last year," Stephen said, his voice a little sharp and high. "We're going to need to delay the start of things until some more officers get here. For now, the media coverage is keeping them at bay."

Marcie and Nicole had made their way over from the gospel

choir in time to hear what Stephen had said. "I'll text our friends and get them over here. We need people to stand up for what's happening." Nicole sounded like she might cry.

"That's fine, Nicole. You do that. But please tell everyone to come only to observe the ceremony. We don't need to start a riot." Stephen was in full-on police mode now.

Nicole nodded, and she, Javier, and Marcie got texting as fast as they could.

I eventually felt strong enough to sit up, and I leaned back against the picnic table. Mom sat beside me and rubbed my thigh.

"Stephen, they recognized me. They were pointing at me," I said.

"Yeah." He patted my knee. "Mary, you might want to go home. Might be safer."

All of me wanted to go home. All of me wanted to slide away and hide. But I saw Sarah's face, saw her watching me, and I thought of that crowd of white men that had killed her mother and then her. If she had been brave enough to stand up to them, I could too. "I'm staying."

I stood up and began walking into the crowd. Marcie caught up to me and tried to hold me back, but I just looked at her and said, "Get the cameras over here." I felt Javier take my hand, and I could sense my other friends behind me. I kept walking. If I stopped, I would run away.

I walked right up to the leader of that bus of racist white men and said, "Did you want to talk to me?"

"You the little lady who started all this. The one with the nigger blood."

I took a deep breath and balled my fists. "I am the young woman with African American ancestry, yes." My story with Moses' cemetery had been big news around here. "What do you want?"

"We wanted to try and talk some sense into you, tell you why you needed to stop this nigger-loving bullshit and come to love your own kind."

All my training in manners, all the southern politeness that had been drilled into me from the day I was born fell away like scales, and I walked up to that man, cleared my throat, and spit in his face. "If you think you're my kind," I said, "you got another think coming." And I turned around and walked straight toward the stage.

Out of the corner of my eye, I could see Sarah, and she was grinning ear to ear. I smiled back until I saw Mom's face behind Sarah's shoulder. This was going to be a conversation later. But now, we had bigger things to worry about.

Suddenly, a crowd of police officers in blue was standing around the stage, and I could see the tips of those red flags moving closer. I also noted that there was a steady stream of teenagers pouring in from Route 60; it looked like my friends' texts had worked. The crowd was getting bigger and bigger, and I was getting more and more scared. This could get ugly fast. Scenes of bodies flying over cars in Charlottesville kept flashing through my mind.

But suddenly, the gospel choir broke into Rhiannon Giddens's song "We Could Fly," and all eyes turned to them. The soloist stood tall just in front of the choir, and her voice soared through us all, cracking open the tension in the air like she'd hit it with a hammer.

"We could fly. We could slip the bonds of earth and rise so high. We could fly across the mountains, together hand in hand. Searching, always searching for the Promised Land."

I looked over, and Sarah had tears on her cheeks, her face turned down the river where she'd sent her mother's body. I looked up at the tree where I'd seen Bo hanging, and then I saw the sky behind it, blue, crisp, clear. For a split second, I thought I saw Bo flying by, a smile lighting up her face. It was probably just a trick of the light and stress, but maybe it was her. I hoped it was.

As soon as the choir finished their song, Mayor Tucker took the mic and welcomed everyone. He made a point of identifying Good Morning America, which I knew was to hinder the white supremacists in our midst as much as anything. He, I was sure, also hoped the media coverage would keep things from getting out of hand.

Then, he began his prepared remarks. He'd shared them with us all earlier, and I couldn't help but be both proud and nervous as he began.

"We are here to remember Beverly Jennings, or Bo as her friends and family called her. Ms. Jennings was a young woman of just thirty-three when she was murdered here in 1928."

I scanned the crowd as the word *murder* echoed silently through them. People shifted, but no one seemed too agitated, not even the men with the flags.

"We are here today for another reason, too, to call out her murder as a lynching, to speak the truth about this horrible event for the first time. I know some of us would rather people keep quiet about these things—some of us want that silence because we have lived through a lot of pain due to the color of our skin, and some of us want that silence because we like to pretend that racism isn't that big a deal. But silence only disguises the wound; it doesn't heal it."

"So I want to bring all the facts to light." He cleared his throat. "My grandfather Gilford Tucker was part of the lynch mob that hung Beverly Jennings on that day in 1928. He, Bucky Sanderson, and Dalford Pope took Ms. Jennings from the county jail, where she awaited trial for a crime she didn't commit, brought her here, and hung her by the neck until she was dead."

The crowd had gone totally silent.

"They claimed that Ms. Jennings had stolen from my grand-daddy's store, that she had stolen flour. Even if that had been the case, which it was not, the crime of theft does not warrant a lynch mob or even a state-sponsored execution. We all know that. But the horror of this crime is made even worse because

Ms. Jennings was falsely accused. She was, in fact, targeted because her daughter Sarah was dating Benjamin Tucker, my great-uncle. The Tuckers had asked Bo to keep Sarah away from Ben, but she's refused. 'Love is love,' that's what she always said."

The silence broke then as a soft murmur began to pass through the crowd, and I scanned quickly to find Johnny Tucker, who had stationed himself with his walker in the middle of the Confederate flag crew. I had really wanted him to look surprised, but all he looked was angry, very, very angry.

"At the time, white people and black people were not legally allowed to date or marry, but we now know that this law was unjust—"

"Do we? Do we really think niggers and white people should have mud children? Really?" The voice came from a man in a button-down shirt and khaki pants who had emerged from behind the Confederate flags. "Don't we all think it's better that we stick with our own kind, even now? And back then, when so-called African Americans were even more uneducated and lazy than they are now, it was totally unreasonable to think that a white boy and a black girl should be together. They were unequally yoked."

I saw a lot of nodding heads in the group of people that had come off the bus, and I could see a large crowd of teenagers—my friends from school—heading toward them, backpacks in hand. This man needed to stop, or there was going to be a riot.

"That's enough, Mr. Keefer." As the mayor said his name, I recognized him. He was one of the most famous white supremacists in the world, one of the coat-and-tie types that was out to give racism a cleaned-up image. I felt bile rise up in my throat.

"We are here for a peaceable memorial service," the mayor continued. "If you can't honor that, then you need to move along." The mayor paused and waited. When no one moved or spoke, he continued. "Today, we remember Beverly Jennings and her daughter Sarah, who was also killed here that day."

Sarah had urged us not to mention Johnny Tucker's presence there that day. She didn't want to put us in danger, and she didn't want to disrupt her mother's service with anything that we didn't have the evidence to support. We all agreed. This was Bo's day, and we wanted her to be the focus.

The mayor continued. "Mrs. Josephine Garrison, Beverly Jennings's descendant, is here to say a few words. Mrs. Garrison."

I had seen pictures of Rosa Parks in her later years; she had been solid, fierce of gaze, and mighty, and it looked like Josephine Garrison was channeling her fortitude. Javier lowered the microphone to her mouth, and she didn't hesitate. "Ninety years ago, three men decided that it was their right to kill my Aunt Bo. They decided that because they didn't like what her daughter did, they would not only make up a crime to accuse her of but they would also exact a sentence of their own making, never mind the court of law. Three men robbed our family of a wonderful woman, and because they decided to murder *her*, my Aunt Sarah died trying to save her mother. Those are the simple facts of this place and the event we remember today."

The crowd was settling again, and I felt my breathing slow.

"But I don't want to give too much time to those murderers. Rather, I want to tell you about Bo. Bo was, by all accounts, the best cook in Terra Linda. The tales I've heard of her peach cobbler would make your mouth water. But not only was she a great cook, she was also a generous one. Anytime someone had a baby, got sick, or had a death in the family, Bo showed up with just the right thing to fill out what everyone else had brought—a big pitcher of tea to go with the fried chicken a neighbor made, or some sweet potatoes cooked to perfect tenderness to go with the greens and turkey another neighbor brought. She had a knack for bringing just the right thing. Some people even said she was magical in this regard."

I looked out over the faces, and everyone was wrapped up in

Mrs. Garrison's words. Even the white supremacists seemed to be listening behind their glowers.

"She could tell a story so well that, my Uncle Joshua said, even the chickens in the yard would stop by to listen, and Mama kept a baby doll that Bo made on her bed until the day she died. She was special. She was somebody's somebody."

Then, Mrs. Garrison looked over her left shoulder at me and gave me a nod and a wink. Suddenly, I realized what she had said. "Uncle Joshua." "Mama." I felt faint.

"She was MY somebody." Mrs. Garrison's voice shook with power. "She was my grandmother."

My eyes scanned the crowd and landed on Johnny Tucker. All the color had slid from his face. He knew what that meant, even if most everybody else didn't.

"My mother was Sarah Jennings, the young girl who was killed here that day as she tried to save her mother from a lynch mob." She took a deep breath. "Most folks don't know that because my mother protected me even all these years after her death. She protected me from what happened to her by telling people I was her brother's child."

I could see the puzzled looks passing amongst the crowd.

"See, all things being equal, I would have been named Josephine Tucker when I was born." She paused, and I watched face after face make the connection. "That's right. My great-grandfather killed my grandmother and my mother."

I whipped my head around to look at Stephen, and he did not look pleased. We had agreed we wouldn't accuse anyone of Sarah's murder, and here, Josephine was doing that very thing.

The mayor and I both moved toward the microphone at the same time. One of us had to stop her before we had a riot, but Josephine bested us.

"I'm not here, though, to accuse anyone. The people who need to know what happened know, and we all carry the weight of that day with us. I don't need a court to decide what is just for me, and I don't need to take justice into my own hands. We all know what using our own definition of justice means. No, what I need today is peace in my spirit, and telling all of you the truth is bringing me that. I am ninety-four years old. I have walked this earth a long time knowing that my mother and grandmother were killed by people who should have loved them. It's time I put that burden down and let you all carry it. Thank you for coming today to honor my grandmother. Thank you for appreciating that she was a person worth honoring, and thank you for hearing and letting the truth of her death change you. That is my hope for all of us today. Thank you."

Stephen and some of his fellow officers were still standing near Johnny Tucker and the men with Confederate flags. They weren't quite in a line to separate them from the rest of the crowd, but they could form one right quick if needed.

Mr. Meade caught my eye, and I looked to Mom, who nodded. I gave Mr. Meade a thumbs up, and he took the stage to share the news that we had raised all the money we needed for the trip to the National Memorial for Peace and Justice as well as to pay for a plaque that would mark this spot as the place of Beverly Jennings's murder.

The choir sang again, "Rise Up, Children" this time, and then, the service was over, and the crowd started to disperse.

Marcie and Nicole met Javier and me by the sycamore, where Sarah and Mrs. Garrison stood. The two women were looking each other in the eye silently. Mrs. Garrison knew better than to speak to a ghost without some cover, but when we came over, she said, "I wanted people to know I claimed you and Grandmama."

"Thank you, Jo. You did good." Sarah reached over and hugged her daughter as the rest of us formed a soft circle around the women so they could have some privacy.

I heard Josephine say, "I love you, Mama," and all the tears I had been holding back streamed silently down my face.

The tender moment didn't last long though. A ruckus had started up over by the stage, and I could see those Confederate flags swaying around as the people who held them moved around. Isaiah and Mom were still on the stage with Mr. Meade, and I could see Shamila and Beatrice just behind them. All of them wore pinched expressions of concern. I grabbed Javier's hand, and we headed that way.

Just as we reached the stage, someone grabbed my arm and spun me around. It was Johnny Tucker, and he looked so mad I thought his head might pop off. His fingers clawed into the flesh above my elbow, and when I tried to wrench my arm away, he dug in deep enough to bruise me. "Listen here, girl. That woman is lying. My brother never fathered no nigger baby, and my daddy only did what he had to do to defend himself. That girl had a knife. You get up there and set the record straight."

I felt Isaiah and Mom come up beside me, and when I glanced over, I saw they were holding hands. Mr. Tucker noticed, too, and his face screwed up into a tight knot.

"Mr. Tucker, take your hand off that young woman. Now." Isaiah's voice was calm but forceful, and Mr. Tucker let my arm go.

He didn't back away though. In fact, he stepped as close to me as his walker would allow and leaned his face right into mine. "You keep stirring up trouble here, Mary Steele, pushing your nose in where it don't belong. Don't be surprised if something doesn't happen to you like happened to that Heather girl in Charlottesville."

I stepped back like I'd been slapped. Heather Heyer had been killed when a white supremacist had driven his car into a crowd in downtown Charlottesville. This man was threatening my life.

That was the last straw with Isaiah. He tugged me backwards gently but decidedly and stepped between me and Mr. Tucker. "Sir, not one more word."

"Or what, you black bastard? What you going to do?"

If the hatefulness wasn't so palpable, the scene would have been funny. Isaiah was in his early fifties, fit, muscular, and Johnny Tucker looked like he'd have trouble opening a jar of mayonnaise. But his rage, his rage was giving him strength. The ache in my arm was a testimony to that.

Isaiah took my hand and then took Mom's, and while I still held onto Javier, we daisy-chained back to the stage where the largest group of police officers was gathered. Stephen gave us a nod, but he was busy trying to keep a fight from breaking out between a group of students and the white supremacists. Things were definitely ramping up.

Mom wanted us to leave, but I didn't think we should. We had, in some sense, started all this, and it felt cowardly to hide from it. So we stayed but back away from the most intense spots in the crowd.

For a half-hour, people shouted at one another, and a few times, it looked like someone was going to throw a punch, but somehow, by the grace of God or the lessons of Charlottesville, no one came to blows. Eventually, the energy dissipated, and people started to wander back to their cars.

We all quietly said goodbye to Sarah and then to Mrs. Garrison and headed home. Marcie suggested we get together at my house, but Mom took one look at me and said, "Tomorrow," before trundling me off toward home.

When we got there, I went right up and changed into my current favorite pj's, hot-pink flannels covered in mugs of hot chocolate. Then, I came down and sat on the couch in the seat closest to the fire and let Mom bring me a real mug of hot chocolate. I had already braced myself because I knew what was coming.

"Mary, I was very proud of you today."

Okay, I hadn't been expecting that.

"No, not for spitting in that man's face—that was simply rude—but for standing up for yourself and for not running away when it got dangerous. You were very courageous."

I did my best to smile, but I mostly felt like crying. "Thanks, Mom."

She shifted closer to me on the couch, and I snuggled against her. "Those things Johnny Tucker said, about Isaiah, about wanting me to end up like Heather Heyer. How can somebody really think that?"

We sat in silence for a long time, and I'd almost drifted to sleep when I heard Mom whisper, "Because they are taught to, Mary. Because they are taught to."

14

*T*he next morning, I woke to the smell of maple sausage and fresh coffee and the sound of voices in the kitchen. I wasn't exactly thrilled to know people were downstairs. I just wanted to sit on the couch and watch DVR'd episodes of *The Magicians* all day.

But then, I heard Marcie say something that made Javier laugh, and I was struck by a wave of FOMO. So I pulled my hair back into a messy bun—an actual messy bun, not the fake cool kind—and headed downstairs.

Everyone was in the kitchen with a mug in their hands, and Isaiah was at the stove with three skillets going—one with that delicious-smelling sausage, one with scrambled eggs, and one with hash browns. My stomach rumbled audibly.

"Good morning," I said as I took a mug out of the cabinet and grabbed the coffee pot. I'd never had a hangover, but I figured it must feel something like the all-body fatigue and ache I was feeling now. I hoped coffee would help.

I took a seat on one of the stools by the peninsula and gave Javier a smile. He leaned over from the stool next to mine and kissed my cheek. "Good morning."

"You ready for some sausage and eggs, Mary?" Isaiah asked

as he turned to me with a smile. He was wearing my mother's flower-covered "Kiss The Cook" apron, and he looked ridiculous. I couldn't help but grin.

"Sure. Sounds good."

Mom came over and began rubbing my shoulders. "You okay? Rough day yesterday."

"Yeah." I wanted to feel sorry for myself, but everyone in the room had been there too. I looked over at Marcie and Nicole, and they looked like death served on a cracker, as my English teacher, Mrs. B., might say. "You guys alright?"

"Tired but just fine," Nicole said. "Shamila texted this morning. She's at the historical society trying to dig up files about Mrs. Garrison. Said we could stop by later if we wanted."

The last thing I really wanted to do was look up anything at all about this. I was tired. I was scared. But the look of expectation on Nicole's face—that girl LOVED research—had me nodding my head before I really knew what I was doing.

"But first, breakfast." Isaiah laid three steaming bowls of food on the table behind me, and we all tucked in. Isaiah was the best cook I knew, but I'd never tell Mom that.

When all the bowls and the coffee pot were empty, Mom told us to head on out. "We'll do the clean-up," she said, draping an arm over Isaiah's shoulder. "Got to teach this man how to work in the kitchen." She quickly dodged his tickling fingers, and I tried to roll my eyes out of my head.

I grabbed my coat off the banister post on the way out. I had seen the heavy frost from outside and didn't want to shiver my way through the day. I pulled the door shut behind us and shoved my hands in my pockets. I felt the mittens I always kept there and some loose change, but there was also a piece of paper. I was always putting things into my pockets so I'd have my hands free, so I figured it was a wrapper or a flyer for something at school. But when I pulled it out, I saw the hand-written words and stopped right in the middle of the driveway.

"I know what you're doing. I know what you see. Mind your own damn business."

I stood there, staring at the white piece of paper with jagged edges. It looked like part of an envelope.

Marcie climbed out of Javier's backseat and read over my shoulder. "Don't move your fingers. We don't want to leave any more fingerprints or obscure evidence." Marcie was a huge fan of all the forensic TV shows.

Someone had been close enough to me to get a note into my pocket. And not just any note. A threatening note. I swiveled my head from side to side, looking to see if the note's writer was nearby, was watching us. But the street was quiet, empty.

I looked at Javier, who was peering out the windshield, and Marcie waved him and Nicole over. We all stood in the driveway staring at the note until Marcie said, "Let's get this inside and into a baggie."

"A baggie?"

"It's evidence."

Right. Evidence. This was a crime. At least I thought it was. Threats were crimes, right?

When the door shut behind us again, Mom and Isaiah turned from the kitchen, where they had The Commodores playing at full blast. One look and the music went off.

"What happened?"

"I found this in my coat pocket." I handed her the note and heard Marcie calling the police. I needed to sit down and collapsed into the sofa. Nicole gently took off my coat and hung it back on the railing.

It is never going to end. That's what I thought. My whole life I was going to be embroiled with hateful people who, even if they didn't say it, thought black people and white people shouldn't mix. I remembered Mrs. Garrison's words about it getting easier, and I thought about how strong she was. I wanted to think I was brave like her, to just accept my gift and use it. But I didn't think

I could. I didn't know if I wanted to. I dropped my head back on the couch and stared at the ceiling.

Stephen and another officer arrived at the house a few minutes later. Stephen was in plainclothes, so I knew that meant he was off-duty. But in a small place like Terra Linda, all the officers know when one of them has a special connection to a case or a family. Someone at the station had called him.

"Mary, can I see the note?"

Marcie handed him the gallon-sized, resealable bag she'd slid the note into.

"Was it in this baggie when you found it?"

"No, we put it in there to preserve the evidence," Marcie said.

A small smile crept into the corner of Stephen's mouth, but he simply said, "Good thinking."

"Any idea when someone put this in your pocket?"

I shook my head. "I wore my coat to school and then to the service, but I have no idea when I last put my hands in my pockets. It could have been there since first period yesterday or only since the end of the gathering last night. I don't know."

"And you don't recognize the handwriting?"

I shook my head.

"Okay, we'll look into it. But I have to be honest. We don't have much to go on."

"What do you mean? You have the type of paper, the jagged edge to compare with what it was torn from, fingerprints, epithelials, handwriting analysis—"

"Marcie, oh, I love your enthusiasm, but we don't have the tools to look for all those things. Plus, you know that not all of what you see on TV is accurate, right?"

Marcie's cheeks colored. "Of course. Sorry, I got carried away."

"Actually, you did say one thing that is feasible. I wonder if anyone would recognize the handwriting. We could post a sample of it on our Facebook page, make up some story about how we found a long lost letter and want to return it. Maybe draw someone out."

"Like an online sting!" Marcie shouted.

Stephen gave her a hard look, and she said, "Sorry. Carried away again." But she still looked giddy.

"I'll get a sample up right away and let you know if we hear from anyone. Until then, Mary, I think it's wisest if you stay close to home. I'll ask patrol cars to swing through the neighborhood more often for the next couple of days."

Mom started to walk the officers to the door, but they all stopped when I said, almost to myself, "Why is someone targeting me?"

Mom gave Isaiah a worried look and then came to sit beside me. "Don't you think that's pretty obvious? You've been involved in all these public events about black people who have been violently killed. Somebody clearly doesn't like that."

"Right, but so have all of you. None of the rest of you got notes, right?"

Everyone looked from one to the other, and then each shook their heads.

"So why me? I didn't even speak last night, and no one but us, Mrs. Garrison, and Mayor Tucker knew we did the memorial because I can see Sarah. Plus, the note says, 'I know what you can see.' It doesn't make sense."

The room got very quiet and very still, and then Isaiah said, "Unless someone hasn't kept your secret, Mary."

My skin went cold. I knew he was right. Someone had not kept the fact that I could see ghosts a secret. I needed to think, so I got up and went up to my room. I knew I was being rude, but I didn't care. Someone had betrayed me, and for the moment, I didn't know who to trust.

It didn't take long for me to rule out all the folks who had been in this with me from the beginning: Javier, Marcie, Nicole, Mr. Meade, Shamila, Beatrice, Isaiah, and of course Mom. I could trust them with my life. I had trusted them with my life. They wouldn't tell a soul.

So it had to be either Mrs. Garrison, the mayor, or Johnny Tucker. Mrs. Garrison had kept the secret of her own ability for most of her ninety-four years. It seemed unlikely that she'd break my confidence, but then, there was always the slightest chance that she actually thought I was butting in where I didn't belong. I hadn't gotten that impression at her house or at the service the day before, but you never know. And Mayor Tucker had seemed so supportive. He'd been completely behind the service, and he'd even confronted his father. It didn't seem likely that he'd tell anyone about me, because who would believe him. Plus, what good would that do him?

So the most logical person to have told was Johnny Tucker. He hadn't even reacted to the fact that Sarah was a ghost though. I'd assumed he hadn't noticed or figured that out, but of course, he had to. You don't just meet someone you saw dead and then not figure out they were a ghost. Right?

What I couldn't figure out was why he'd told. Sure, maybe he was trying to discredit me—a good possibility—but I imagined that most people would think an old man who saw ghosts wasn't quite right in the head anymore. Wouldn't it hurt his credibility more than mine if he went around telling people that Sarah's ghost haunted the old lock?

I spent most of that day in my room. Javier and Marcie texted a few times, and I responded with emoticons just so they wouldn't worry. But I didn't feel like talking.

Mom brought me lunch, grilled cheese and tomato soup, and she let me be until dinner time. By then, I was feeling pretty lonely, and I was no closer to understanding the motivation behind the note or who had placed it in my pocket. Plus, I'd begun wondering what exactly it was I needed to do to help Sarah move on and be done with all this mess. Clearly, the memorial service had not been enough, but I couldn't get a hand on what else I needed to do. And truthfully, I didn't much care. I was tired, and I was angry, and I was scared. I wanted to forget I'd ever seen a ghost and go back to being a teenage bookworm with a few good friends and no popularity of any sort.

When Mom came to get me for dinner, I huffily climbed out from under my covers, pulled on my ripped Doctor Who sweatshirt, and went downstairs.

I half-expected to see Isaiah there, but instead, it was just Mom, a big bowl of macaroni and cheese, and a chicken Caesar salad. She knew me so well.

We ate in silence, but when Mom brought me a piece of chocolate chip cookie cake and a cup of peppermint tea, she said, "Let's talk."

With Mom, it was never a question. Her work as a therapist taught her that people often needed to be pushed to share, and it was especially true with me since I didn't ever want to give her another person's problems to worry about. She always tells me it's different because I am her daughter, but still . . .

Tonight, though I didn't even try to pretend I was okay, because I wasn't. I was terrified. And tired. Even more tired than terrified.

"Why does this keep happening? And why to me?"

"Are you talking about the threat or about seeing ghosts?"

Good question. I stared into my mug. "Both I think. I mean I know it's supposed to be a gift that I can see these people, that I can help them move on. But I don't get instructions, and I'm not Melinda Gordon. I just don't have the, the, the . . . what's the word?"

"Resilience?"

"Yeah, I don't have her resilience." Mom and I had watched every episode of *The Ghost Whisperer* a dozen times or more. At first, it had been kind of fun to compare myself to Jennifer Love Hewitt's character. But the more I watched, the more I realized I was learning, trying to get down exactly what made it possible for Melinda to, week after week, send people into the light. I felt like she had it easy though. . . . For her, all it took was a conversation. It was like she was a translator, relaying messages back and forth. But I didn't get away with just telling people what someone said. My "gift" didn't work like that.

"She did get threatened though, right? And people thought she was crazy? Plus, she had professional writers, and after five seasons, she got to quit." Mom gave me a soft smile.

"Maybe if someone could dress me for each encounter: get me out of my flannel shirts into velvet coats and gauzy skirts . . ." I took a big bite of my cookie. "Nah."

We sat for a moment, and then Mom took my hand. "Maybe what we need is just to focus on what we can do. I mean, we don't know who sent that note, and we don't even really know what it means. Maybe it just means this person knows you can see the high school from your bedroom window. . . . Never mind, that's even more creepy." She shook her head quickly. "But we can focus on how to help Sarah move on, right? Any ideas about that?"

"Not really." I took another bite of cookie cake. "Okay, well, I did think of one thing."

Mom nodded.

"A family reunion."

"Of Sarah's family?"

"Yes, including the Tuckers. I don't know. It seems important somehow to bring them together." I remembered the feel of the note in my hands. "But . . ."

"But you think it might have been Johnny Tucker who wrote that note."

"If not him, then . . ."

"Okay, Stephen is on that. He'll definitely look into Johnny. Let's focus on this reunion idea, keep our head in the game on what we can do."

I could have protested, could have told Mom that I was too scared to do anything, could have told her that it would do no good. But she knew I was scared, and she also knew that I wouldn't quit, no matter how much I wanted to. It was too important. So I just took the shortcut. "Okay, so what do we do?"

"Well, let's make a family tree and see who we need to invite." She took a legal pad out of the kitchen drawer, and I opened her laptop to Ancestry.com. We put our heads down to work.

By the time we were done, we'd had the family trees all plotted from both Beverly Jennings's and Gilford Tucker's sides. In total, we had at least sixty-six people spanning five generations. The oldest family members were definitely Josephine Garrison and Johnny Tucker, and it sounded like—from a quick phone call to Mrs. Garrison—that the youngest was little Jodi, Mrs. Garrison's great-granddaughter, who was five months old.

"That's a good-size reunion," Mom said. "Mrs. Garrison is sure we could have it up in the hollow where she grew up?"

"That's what she said. She said there's a big field at the top of the lane that everybody uses for barbecues and such. She seemed sure we could use it. Sounded like she was going to start phone calls right away to let folks know to stay tuned for more info."

"Well, then we better get planning. Feel up to having everyone over tomorrow?"

"Do you? I mean other people have houses, and we could go to one of theirs."

"No, no, I like having everyone here. It makes me feel hospitable. Plus, then, we clean."

We spent the rest of the evening sending texts to catch everyone up and set a meeting for two the next afternoon. I was put on dusting duty, which wasn't as awful as usual because at least I was busy doing something instead of worrying. It's hard to really fret when you have to pick up the billion candles your mom has on every surface of the house.

$\mathcal{M}$rs. Garrison arrived first, hat in hand from church. We'd invited her over for lunch, but she'd reminded us that black church didn't get out right at twelve, so she'd just come over when the service finished. She was early, but not by much.

"I'm so excited about this reunion, Mary," she said as she took a seat on our couch. Her feet didn't quite touch the floor, but I thought it might embarrass her if I brought the step stool from the kitchen, so I tried not to stare at them dangling there. "We've had reunions before, of course, but never with the Tuckers invited."

"Aren't you nervous that they might actually come? To make trouble if not to actually acknowledge that you're kin?" I asked, my memory of the note still fresh.

"Not really." She shrugged. "What are a few racist white people going to do in a large group of black people?"

My mouth dropped open. "Guns, Mrs. Garrison."

"Child, you think white people the only ones who carry guns?" She gave me a sideways grin, and I felt myself relax for the first time since the previous morning. "Let's talk about the important stuff: the food."

"What kind of food would you like us to bring?"

She let out a hard breath. "Mary, you haven't been to many family reunions, have you?"

I wilted a bit. "No. It's always just been Mom and me."

"I know." Her voice was soft. "I read your story a few months back. Hard thing." Then she smiled again. "But we're going to break you in the right way. At a proper family reunion, it's potluck. Everyone brings their favorite. We have a couple of tables for the main courses, and we have an equal number of tables for the desserts." She winked at me.

"Don't you end up with lots of the same thing."

"Of course, but that's just an opportunity to decide which you like better—macaroni and cheese with that crunchy top or the creamy stuff? Green beans steamed and mixed with almonds or cooked until totally soft with fatback? It's like a culinary adventure at a good family reunion, and ours will be good."

It had been a few hours since Mom and I had made grits and bacon, and I was starving. I could almost feel my mouth watering as I imagined all those tables full of food.

Soon, everyone else arrived, and we piled plates high with Chinese take-out and did our usual lounging around the living room. Mrs. Garrison ate without dropping a grain of rice from her chopsticks while looking like she was holding fine china rather than a leftover Easter plate. Before long, I even forgot to worry about whether or not she was feeling comfortable.

The meal completed, Mom said, "Mrs. Garrison, would you mind telling us what you'd like for your family reunion?"

For a second I thought Mrs. Garrison was going to stand, but then, she just sat up a little taller and said, "Really, I'd prefer things be pretty simple. Good food—Mary and I have already talked about that—lots of time for people to talk together, maybe a little presentation about our family tree. Some folks like to have dancing and such, but I prefer something simple for an afternoon."

"I'd be happy to do a family tree presentation, Mrs. Garrison, if you'd like," Shamila said. A smile flashed upon Mrs. Garrison's face. "Do you or other members of your family have any photographs I could use in a slide show?"

I reached down and picked up the photo of Benjamin and Sarah from the coffee table. "Could we use this one? Or is that just weird?"

I looked from Mrs. Garrison to Shamila. And Shamila looked at Mrs. Garrison. "I think it would be a nice addition, but I can understand if you'd rather not," Shamila said.

"Goodness, no. It's fine to use the picture. That's part of our story . . . and the part that brings the Tuckers and the Jennings together after all. Not including it would be like putting together a puzzle and finding you were missing one piece." Mrs. Garrison stood then. "I feel confident you all have this well in hand, but I best be getting on now. I have been out a long time, and I'm feeling tired. Plus, at my age, it's best not to even be near the road as night approaches. Thank you kindly for having me."

I glanced at the clock on the mantel and smiled. It was three thirty in the afternoon.

I walked her to the door, and she gave me one of those rib-cracking hugs before making her way to her very new and very large Lincoln Continental.

It didn't take us long to get the rest of the details ironed out. April 22, a Sunday afternoon, starting at two—or whenever people got out of church—at the large field up Mrs. Garrison's hollow, which, Mr. Meade had figured out, was beside where Beverly Jennings's house used to stand. Isaiah had confirmed with the neighbors that it was okay to hold the reunion there. Now, we just needed an invitation to send out.

Fortunately, Marcie had already created an evite, and Mrs. Garrison had loaned me her address book with far more emails than I expected a ninety-four-year-old woman to have. It looked like we were all set.

As Javier began to gather up the plates and head to the kitchen, Beatrice asked, "Will we want media coverage?"

I puffed up my cheeks and let out a long breath. Good question. Media coverage would help us make sure things stayed under control, like they had at the memorial service, but it also meant that I'd be in the spotlight again. I didn't know if I wanted even more attention, especially with this threat.

"Let's ask Mrs. Garrison when we see her tomorrow. She invited Mary and me over for tea after school. I'll check with her then." Leave it to Mom to save me the embarrassment of having to make the decision about me.

"Sounds good," Beatrice said.

Everyone but Javier gathered their things and headed toward the door. Marcie came over and gave me a hug. "You okay?" she asked.

"Yep, right as rain."

She shook her head. "No, you're not, but that's okay. See you tomorrow. Text me if you need me."

I gave her a wan smile. Good friends get it.

Mom had invited Javier to stay for dinner and a movie, and I was grateful for the distraction. We had scrambled-egg sandwiches and watched one of those hokey Hallmark movies. In this one, a young producer goes to a small town, where apparently everyone knew how to do elaborate flower displays on their front porches, to film a segment about a local man who cares for abandoned basset hounds. While she's there, she meets the man's son, and well, it all works out in the end. Javier's a romantic at heart, but he was being a supremely good sport to watch this formulaic nonsense. He used the five snide remarks that Mom and I allotted him very wisely.

By the time he left, after giving me a gentle kiss on the front porch, I was feeling a little more calm, a little less tight in the shoulders.

I helped Mom clean up the popcorn bowls and the hot cocoa mugs and told her goodnight. I texted Marcie to say that I was okay. I checked Facebook and Insta then climbed into bed.

I had just drifted off when I heard glass shatter and then a whoosh pass through my room. By the time I opened my eyes, my curtains were on fire. I grabbed at them—for no reason that made any sense—only to burn my hands and then screamed for Mom; at the same time, I ran to the kitchen for our one and only fire extinguisher.

She was already in my room beating the curtains with a rug when I got back there, and between the two of us, we were able to put out the flames and stomp out the small puddle of fire that had formed at the foot of my bed. Unfortunately, I stomped with my bare foot and got glass embedded in it.

Someone on the street must have seen the flames because a firetruck rolled up moments after we got the fire out, and Mom met them outside. The chief asked to come in and look at the scene to see what caused it, and he took one look at the burnt spot on the rug and the glass bottle neck by my dresser and said someone had thrown a Molotov cocktail through my bedroom window.

I had already figured out that was what had happened, but having an official word on the cause somehow made it all the more real. I felt all the blood drain out of my body as I collapsed into the big wing-backed chair in the corner of my room. *Not again.*

It took a while for the fire company to be sure everything was out. I sat in the back of an ambulance as a paramedic tended my burned hands and cleaned out the cut on my foot. By the time she was done, I had a dozen text messages, and Javier was back. The volunteer fire company in our small Virginia town often relies on some high school students for staffing. One of them had apparently been unable to resist the urge to share the story on Facebook, and so my phone was blowing up and my boyfriend was fuming.

"We've been through this before, Mary, but this is ridiculous. It was your bedroom. What if you'd been deep asleep? What if . . ." He took a deep breath. "Are you okay?"

I held up my bloody left foot and said, "I'll live." But then, I felt a cold chill wash over me.

"How did they know that was my bedroom? I mean there are," I looked up at the house and counted, "four windows on the second story of the house. How did they know that one was mine?"

Javier furrowed his brow and sat down next to me. "Good question."

"I think I can answer that." I looked up to see my friend Blanch, and that cold chill was replaced with a gentle, warm glow. He, almost as much as Javier, always had my back.

"Blanch!" I started to jump up and hug him, but he caught me by the shoulder and looked at my foot before leaning down to me. "What are you doing here?"

"I am in the police training academy over in Lexington, but this week, I'm shadowing Stephen, I mean, Officer Douglas." I looked toward where Blanch pointed and saw Stephen talking with the fire chief.

"Well, I'm glad you're here. Seems like you always show up when I need the most help."

He blushed, and I felt—rather than saw—Javier roll his eyes next to me.

"You said you had a theory on how they knew which window was mine?"

"Right." He reached into his back pocket and pulled out a piece of folded paper. "I found this on Dad's kitchen table tonight."

He handed me the paper, and I unfolded it. It was a flyer of sorts with my yearbook picture from last year at the top of the page. Below it were the words, "She's At It Again!" Then, they listed my home address, and there was a sketch of my house with a hand-drawn arrow pointing right at my window. The bottom of the flyer said, "You know what to do!"

If I hadn't been living this moment, I would have thought this was too over the top to be real, but my foot definitely hurt, and I was definitely in an ambulance with my two friends standing over me.

"They're targeting her and publicizing it?" Javier looked like his head might pop off his neck in anger.

"Appears so. Stephen says a couple of people have brought these flyers to him today, concerned about what might happen. They didn't think it was serious though, just a bunch of talk. Guess he was wrong." I sighed.

"Who brought them in? I mean, if they had them, they had to know where they came from, right?"

"Probably, but they only gave statements under promise of anonymity, so Stephen won't even tell me who they are."

I stood up, ready to march over and demand Stephen tell me who these people were, but the minute my foot hit the pavement, I screamed and crumpled.

Mom, ever calm, walked over and gave Blanch a hug. He then filled her in. She looked at me. "I'll go talk to Stephen. You," she looked pointedly at my foot, "go on inside and get that foot up. Gentlemen, will you please help Mary inside?"

Javier didn't even give Blanch a chance to move. He just scooped me into his arms and carried me up the sidewalk. I was surprised, not by this act of chivalry—Javier could be a little jealous—but by his strength. He only had an inch or two on me, and I definitely outweighed the thin fellow. But adrenaline and bravado can do miraculous things, I suppose.

Blanch followed us, and when we got to the door, Marcie and Nicole were already on the porch. Javier put me down, and Marcie took my other shoulder while Nicole opened the door. I hopped to the couch. It was just past midnight, and I hoped we'd all be excused from school the next day.

I told everyone what happened, and Blanch took notes. He was taking this police thing pretty serious, I figured. He passed around the note and said, "Have any of you seen a flyer like this before tonight?"

Marcie laughed and said, "Blanch, a black lesbian and her

girlfriend and a Mexican guy who's dating the girl on the flyer. Really?"

Color flooded Blanch's face again, but he laughed. "Right. So that's a no."

"You said this was at your dad's? He's still mixed up with these guys?"

"Not exactly. But they want him to be. What Mary and you all have been doing—"

"And you, too, Blanch," Nicole said. He blushed again.

"What we've been doing, it's getting people all riled up. Lots of people want these things to stay secret."

"But they say it's about privacy, about not dredging up old wounds." Isaiah hung his coat on the door. "They claim civility and etiquette as ways to avoid truth. Nonsense." He looked like he could spit nails.

I could hear the fire in my friends' voices, and I wanted to feel it, too, wanted to latch onto that sense of justice that kept rising up in me. But tonight, I was just scared. I just wanted to know that Mom and I were safe.

Shamila and Beatrice came in then. "The fire came over the scanner," Beatrice said, "so I called Shamila and Tom." Mr. Meade was right behind them.

"The gang's all here," Mom said as she came in with Stephen Douglas.

The requisite hot cocoa was made, and someone—Nicole maybe—tucked me into the couch with a blanket and handed me a couple of ibuprofen. I could feel how tired I was, but I knew sleep wasn't coming soon. I kept seeing that flyer and then the flames flash through my head.

"Okay, I have a plan," Mr. Meade said after everyone was settled around the room. "What if we created a whole bunch of flyers that look just like this one but spread love and truth instead."

I heard Javier and Blanch snicker, but Mr. Meade pinned them with that infamous teacher stare and said, "I know it sounds all unicorns and fairy tales, but hear me out. The idea is to confuse people, dilute the waters of the white supremacists a bit. We'll put images of other Terra Linda buildings on the flyers and include facts and stories about all the great things that happened here. Like, we'll show the courthouse and talk about how Gary and Stephen Limus were the first gay couple to marry in town, and we'll do one with the library and talk about how many kids go to story time each week. Stuff like that."

The more Mr. Meade explained his plan to create and disseminate these flyers, the more I thought it could work, at least to help confuse people or dilute the power of the "real" flyers if not to actually spread love and truth. I did appreciate Mr. Meade's idealism though.

"No one else will target your house though, will they? I mean, after all this." Javier pointed out the window to all the police cruisers and firetruck lights outside. He immediately looked a little sheepish. "I'm being naïve, aren't I?" He looked at Mom. She'd told him and me often enough that we had too much faith in people's goodness. And you'd think that with all that we'd been through in the past few months, we'd know that, . . . but clearly, idealism dies hard in some of us.

Stephen spoke up. "Unfortunately, I think it's very possible. Someone knew which room was yours and cared enough to make these flyers, Mary, and so that means someone is very focused on getting you to be quiet."

In all the hubbub about the flyers, I had lost track of the fact that someone had to know about our house to be able to print the flyer in the first place. I shivered under the blanket.

"In fact, I'd like to move you all to a safe house," Stephen said, and he wasn't asking.

I immediately thought of all the seedy rooms in the TV procedurals Mom and I watched, but one look at her told me that the decision had been made. "Go pack a bag," she said.

The firetrucks stayed on the scene at Stephen's request so that they could be a distraction while Mom and I got into the back of his police cruiser and headed off. We didn't know where we were going, and we weren't allowed to tell even the people at the house with us. It was too easy for someone, even our best friends, to slip up and tell the wrong person.

Stephen planned to put a patrol car on our street for the next few days just to keep an eye on things and to, hopefully, prevent our house from burning down. But we'd be away, safe, we hoped.

The logistics of being kept in protective custody—turned out my extensive knowledge of police TV had actually taught me a true phrase—were tricky, even if my assumptions about the place we'd be staying were off. They actually put us up in one of the swanky Victorians downtown. Not seedy at all.

Each morning, Stephen came and picked me up in his personal car and dropped me off at school, knowing I'd be safe there since visitors were closely monitored. Then, he picked me up after school and took me back to the safe house.

This all felt a little much, but two nights later, when a car drove by, shot out our living room windows with a hunting rifle, and then sped off before the officer on duty could even get the plate, we were grateful. Very grateful.

The next morning, I was surprised to see Blanch talking to the principal outside my homeroom, and when he caught up to me as I headed to first period, I learned he was my protective detail. I was feeling very "witness to a mob hit" famous, and I didn't really like it. But clearly, Stephen didn't think school was that safe anymore.

Fortunately, no one took much notice of Blanch after he told a few key blabbermouths that he was doing a special investigation into the sale of ADD meds. Plus, he blended right back in with his old crew, and it seemed like some people forgot he had ever graduated. But the way he was always where I was, not right with me but nearby between every class and at lunch, sure made him stand out to me. I mean he and I were friends, but really, this was a bit much.

And Javier liked it even less than I did.

By Friday afternoon, I was sure that Stephen's wariness was unwarranted. I was about to tell Blanch to go ahead on home because the day was almost over, when I stepped into the bathroom on the second floor by Mr. Meade's history classroom before last period. Blanch was in the hallway just outside, pretending to ask Mr. Meade about drug use, when an arm caught me around the throat and pulled me into the wheelchair-accessible stall at the back.

When I looked up, I saw a white girl, no a woman really, with long black hair that was clearly dyed and bad painful-looking sores on her face. A meth user, no doubt. In a small mountain town like ours, you know a crank user when you see one. This woman was rail-thin, and she looked like she'd lived a hard eighty years in the body of a thirty-year-old. Weak, though, she was not, and as she pinned me against the stall door by the throat.

I struggled against her grip, trying everything from biting to kicking to getting enough air to scream. But then she held up a knife and put its tip just below my ribs. I stopped moving immediately.

"Listen, Mary Steele. Nobody wants you messing with this stuff anymore. No more stirring up ancient history. No more ceremonies or press conferences. No more talking to ghosts." The way her mouth pinched at that last bit made me think she was reciting something, something she didn't really believe.

"If you don't stop, you and your mother will have a permanent place to reside in Terra Linda with a really nice sign above your heads, if you know what I mean."

I shivered.

"Now, tell me you're going to back off and go back to a normal teenager's life. Listen to Miley Cyrus. See movies with that pretty boyfriend of yours. Leave all this alone . . . for good."

I still wasn't getting much air, so the idea of saying anything was absurd, not to mention that I couldn't stop talking to ghosts if I wanted to. So I just stared at her.

I felt the knife move a little further into the folds of my skin, so I opened my mouth and was about to speak when a large hand came under the door of the stall and yanked the woman's foot out from under her. She fell back and hit her head on the toilet paper holder, and I scrambled to unlock the door and leap into Blanch's arms.

I took several long breaths as he put the woman in handcuffs, and then I asked, "How did you know?"

"Mary, you pee quick. It was taking too long."

I didn't explore any further how he had knowledge of my peeing speed because I was so grateful, and because now, adrenaline fading, I could barely stand up. Blanch texted Marcie, who came running from her French class on the floor below, and the four of us walked to the office and waited for Stephen to arrive.

Marcie let Javier and Nicole know what was going on but told them to stay in their classes after I said I couldn't handle any more attention. It was only that night at the safe house when Stephen and Blanch came by—just as Mom and I sat down to watch *MacGyver* and eat the sugar cookies she'd made—that I learned Blanch had given my friends a heads up to keep their phones on vibrate in case he texted. Clearly, everyone had been more concerned about me than I had been.

Stephen said the woman had multiple arrests for methamphetamine use—as I had suspected she would—and that she had told him someone paid her $1,000 to threaten me. She wouldn't tell him who hired her though, said it would put her life in danger.

"As if meth wasn't already doing that," I said and sighed. "I kind of feel sorry for her."

"Mary Steele, she could have killed you." Blanch was having none of my tender heart tonight.

"I know, but she was just desperate." I needed to focus on someone besides myself.

Mom brought the kettle over and refilled everyone's tea mugs. "But if this woman feared for her life, she wasn't hired by some nobody. Whoever threatened her must have some power."

I hadn't thought of that, but clearly Stephen had. "Exactly. Unfortunately, as you well know, a lot of the most influential men in our town are tied up with white supremacist organizations or if not officially linked, share a lot of those groups' beliefs. It could be a lot of people."

My mind raced back to the woman's face as she recited her spiel. "'No more talking to ghosts.' That's what she'd said. Whoever hired her knows." I felt my heart start to race.

"Well, we figured that, right? After the flyers. Clearly, it's the same person."

Suddenly, it came to me. I knew who it was, and it wasn't Johnny Tucker. But there was no value saying so until I could prove it. I tried to keep my face neutral, and slowly, I began leaning over my mug and resting more and more of my body on the table. I knew that saying I was tired would launch red flags into my mom's mind since I never said I was tired, so I had to act like I was still interested but signal that I was waning.

Worked like a charm. "Mary's had enough today, guys," she said as she put a hand on my shoulder. "Thanks for everything. Thanks, Blanch, for saving my girl." Mom gave him a hug.

The guys left, and Mom walked me to the little bedroom I was using, tucked me in, kissed my cheek, and turned off the light.

I gave her a few minutes to move away, and then I took out my phone and started texting. We had an attempted murderer to catch, and it wasn't going to be easy.

$\mathcal{T}$he next morning, I convinced Mom to let me go downtown to a coffee shop to meet Marcie, Nicole, and Javier. I had invited Blanch along after swearing him to secrecy via text the night before, and so she caved, nervously.

"I guess you could use some time to just relax with your friends. Okay, but I want you to text me every half hour."

"Okay, Mom. But no one will know where I am except you and my friends. I'll be totally fine."

"That's what you said about school."

She had a point.

We all met at ten a.m. at the coffee shop on Main Street in Lexington. Everyone got their various skinny, tall, mocha-choca beverages and sat down at a corner table. Blanch insisted on facing the wall and putting me between him and the corner—a request which made Javier twitch until he took the chair beside me and also my hand.

"I know who is doing all this." I blurted before anyone could swallow their first sip.

Everyone looked at me like I'd suddenly said, "I love Smurfs."

"I know who made the fliers."

Still puzzled faces. Blanch leaned forward and said softly, "Right, Mary. We all know it's Johnny Tucker."

"Nope." I was feeling a bit smug.

Marcie gave me a forceful stare that someone might even call a glare.

"Okay, then who do you think it is?" Nicole said.

"Mayor Tucker."

My friends exchanged glances and then looked back at me. "What are you talking about, Mary? He was all in favor of the memorial, and he even admitted that his own grandfather had killed Beverly and Sarah," Javier said.

"I know. But hear me out. What if all of that was a cover? What if he was just pretending to be in support when really what he wanted was minimize exposure of his family's history?"

"I guess that could make sense," Marcie said. "I mean, before, that ceremony would have meant we backed off because we would have done what we needed to do to send the ghost on. But now, Sarah is still here, and we don't know why."

"Exactly!" My voice got a little loud, and I blushed when the barista glanced our way. "Clearly, there is something else going on here, something else that's keeping Sarah tethered, and I think it's that something that is making Mayor Tucker threaten me."

Blanch looked puzzled. "Okay, I can definitely see what you mean about someone wanting to silence you before the big secret comes out, but why do you think it's the mayor? Couldn't it be his dad or someone else altogether?"

"It could, but the mayor is the only other person who knows I can see ghosts." I let my words sit down hard at the table.

Even though I felt sure about my theory, I wilted a bit under the sadness of that revelation. I had so loved that someone powerful in our town was on the good side for once.

"There is another possibility," Marcie said, and I gave her a skeptical glance. "He could have told someone else."

"Well, that's another kind of betrayal, isn't it?" Nicole cut in.

"I mean, after what happened with his dad, surely he knew that he shouldn't be telling anyone else." She looked at me for confirmation, and I nodded. "So he betrayed Mary's trust."

"Yeah, but that's a lesser level of betrayal, isn't it?" Marcie said. "To tell one person is better than to initiate a hate campaign."

Nicole's voice was getting louder. "Not necessarily. Not if the person he told was bent on hatred, not if he wasn't wise about who he told."

Javier stood up. "We may be getting a little off-track here in this philosophical debate about the hierarchy of betrayal."

I smiled up at him. I had been about to say the same thing.

"Why don't we just go talk to the mayor?" Javier suggested.

I was on my feet and putting on my jacket in a flash, but I was surprised to see Marcie and Nicole still sitting there and giving each other a look of concern.

"What!"

"Mary, you need to think. If he is the one who started all this —either by launching the hate campaign himself or by telling someone who did—don't you think it might be a little dangerous to just pull up to his house and confront him." Marcie was leaning toward me, a wrinkle of concern between her eyes.

I dropped back into my seat. I had always been a person who preferred to make the quick decision rather than to have to sit with the discomfort of trying to decide—Mom said that made that trait made me a J, not a P, on the Myers-Briggs scale. But sometimes, even I had to admit that quick action wasn't always the right action.

Javier didn't sit down.

"She's right, Javier," Blanch said.

Javier threw Blanch a grin and said, "I know. But we're already on it." Then Javier showed me his phone. Stephen had texted to say he was on his way to the mayor's house right now, and he'd wait for us before going to the door.

I was back on my feet again as Blanch said, "Plus, I have

this," and pulled back his lined flannel shirt to show us what looked like a men's razor.

"Planning on shaving someone?" Nicole said.

"It's a Taser, Nic. I'm not allowed to carry a gun yet, but I passed my training for this yesterday."

I glanced at Marcie as she put on her jacket, and she let out a snicker. Then, I giggled, and soon all of us but Blanch were having a hard time catching our breath from the laughter.

"What? What's so funny?" Blanch's face was getting red.

"Oh, Blanch, just the image of you saying, 'Stop. Police.' And then drawing down with a Taser." Javier had just enough air to explain.

Blanch looked a little stricken, but almost instantly, a turn appeared at the corner of his mouth, and soon, he was doubled-over in laughter too.

We bussed our table and headed out the door. But as soon as I reached the street, the smile dropped from my lips. There, lined up on the other side of the road, were a bunch of men with pickup trucks bearing Confederate flags on their beds. Every single one of their faces were looking right at me.

I shuddered, glanced behind me, and made a decision. "Not today, jackasses. Not today," I said under my breath.

Mom is always talking about "the good old days" when people weren't always on their phones and didn't expect to hear from someone instantaneously. But today, I expected she was glad we all had these "mini-computers" in our pockets because as soon as we saw the men, my friends and I were texting as fast as our little thumbs could move. Javier texted Stephen. I got hold of Mom by phone, and she said she'd tell Isaiah, Shamila, and Beatrice. Nicole reached out to Mr. Meade, and Blanch jumped on Facebook to tell people to get to downtown Lexington right away.

I made a second phone call—to Mrs. Garrison. I wanted her to know what was happening, just in case someone came to her house. She was totally unfazed. "Oh, child, remember what I said about black people carrying guns. They just need to try me." I laughed at the image of this tiny woman with a big black pistol, but I knew she was serious. She was not trifling with racists or with her family history.

We all went back inside and took the same table after ordering more drinks. Manners dictated buying something if we were going to take up space, even we took it to save our own lives. Southern runs deep.

Within minutes, friends of ours from school were filling the coffee shop, and soon thereafter, we heard Stephen's cruiser, sirens blaring, pull up on the street. I got up to peek out the front window, but the men across the street hadn't moved. In fact, I thought there were more of them, all leaning back casually on the cars and trucks parked there.

Stephen came in and headed right for our table. "Glad you texted, Javier. The mayor had seen me outside his house and was just headed my way when I got your message. I let him know what was happening, and he's on his way too."

I groaned. "He may be the one who started all this."

"I don't think so. He looked appalled when I told him what was going on here. Surprised, too."

I still had my doubts, but what was done was done, and we had a bigger issue on our hands at the moment. "You can't just make them go away, can you?"

"I wish I could, but they are on public property, and they're allowed to lean against their own vehicles all they want. They'll just argue they were taking in the scenery, I expect."

"Aren't they blocking traffic or something?"

"Not really. They're standing in the bike lane, so cars have plenty of room, . . . however. . ." Stephen's face took on a sinister grin, and I felt a shiver of pleasure run through me. Sometimes, activism could be fun.

Within minutes, we had let everyone we could know that we needed LOTS of bicycles in Lexington as soon as possible.

Javier made another trip to the window. "More of them now. They must be calling in reinforcements too."

"I feel like we're in one of those old Westerns where everyone is lining up for the shootout at high noon," Nicole said.

"There'll be no shooting today if I can help it," Blanch said and flashed his Taser again, a huge grin on his face.

We all collapsed in laughter, well, all of us except Stephen who just looked puzzled.

Mom and Isaiah arrived and Mom said, "We would have been here sooner, but there were so many bicycles on 60." She scanned our faces when Blanch gave me a high five. "What?"

"It's working." I explained our plan.

By now, even the coffee shop staff was aware of the situation, and they started handing out free coffee to anyone we talked to, and when Shamila and Beatrice arrived, they gave them each HUGE lattes. Allegiances were clear here, as one would expect. Many a movement had started behind a cup of coffee.

Eventually, we gave up all pretense of trying to relax, and we went to stand by the window, the line of us mirroring the line of them across the way.

"What we've got ourselves here, folks, is a standoff," Marcie said in a nasal voice, and we all laughed again. Laughter, I have learned, is often the best thing in the face of great fear.

The line of men kept growing longer and longer down Main Street, and I found myself marveling at how many white men were willing to step out as overtly racist in front of the entire city. I mean, it was one thing to do something racist—like call the neighborhood security officers on a black woman and her family at your community pool—when you think no one will really know. But to stand out here in broad daylight . . .

Of course, these men drove around with Confederate flags on their trucks. There was no way you did that now and claimed simple "Southern pride." That flag signaled racism 100 percent whether you wanted to own up to that or not.

Just then, I saw Mayor Tucker come through the shop door,

and I stepped back behind Javier and Blanch. I didn't know what —if anything—he'd done, but I was already feeling at my limit with confrontation for one day.

But I didn't need to worry, Marcie was up to the task. She walked right over to him and started talking. She was pointing, and I could see the pink coming into her cheeks. I couldn't hear what she was saying, but she wasn't going easy on him.

To his credit, the mayor looked pretty sheepish. He hung his head and nodded a lot. Once it was his turn to speak, he said something, and Marcie let out a long breath. Then, she pointed over at us and started walking, with the mayor, our way.

He didn't hesitate a minute before speaking. "I'm sorry, Mary. I thought my dad had not picked up on you seeing Sarah, but I guess he did and asked some of the folks in town and found out that you've seen other ghosts too. You have, right? I mean, at the cemetery and in that school? There was someone dead there, too, right?" It wasn't a secret, this ability of mine, but I didn't tell the newspaper or anything. Still, in a small town . . . .

I nodded.

"I'm so sorry," the mayor continued. "I really didn't think he would take it this far."

I could have gotten mad, shouted, vented out all the fear I had in that moment. And part of me really wanted to do that. But the other part of me—the part that knew that even the best intention can go really wrong—knew that would do no good, and that we'd go further with forgiveness than with anger. So I said, "It's okay. We can't control what other people do." I took a deep breath. "But I'm glad you're here."

The look of relief on the mayor's face was a gift to me, and when he reached out to shake my hand, I hugged him. Then I asked, "Now, what do we do?"

"Now, we go out and face these bastards." The mayor was looking out the window, and I could imagine him putting his hands to his hips to check his pistols like in those old Westerns.

I grinned. There was something so great about when adults, especially polished adults, swore.

"But let me do one thing first. I'll be right back." We watched him walk out of the coffee shop and cross the street. He leaned in a car window, and a minute later, Johnny Tucker stood up on the other side. He'd been hiding in his car.

"Coward," I said out loud.

"I couldn't agree more," my mom said.

I smiled.

Mayor Tucker gave us a little wave, and we found ourselves leading a long line of people out of the coffee shop. A steady stream of bikes was still flowing by, and the men had been forced to step back between the cars instead of forming a wall of hatred along them.

"The power of social media," Mr. Meade said.

Soon, we were lined up, hand-in-hand along the sidewalk on our side of the street, and I could see more and more people joining us as word spread about what was happening. Main Street is long and hilly, and our line was beginning to creep up the hill to my left. I didn't exactly understand what was happening, and I wasn't sure everyone who was joining knew just what was going on. But still, my chest felt warm, and I began to think everything might just be alright.

As we continued to stand, the men with the Confederate flags mirrored our line-up on their side, and sadly, a few people came to stand beside them too. I imagined they were thinking about how hard they had it; jobs were scarce around here, and many of our neighbors, black and white, had to scrounge for grocery money. Many of my friends had lost their electricity when their parents couldn't pay the electric bill. So I knew that when people talked about white privilege, they often bristled because it didn't seem like they were privileged at all, . . . and somehow, that Confederate flag had become a symbol for all that. The irony, of course, was that that battle flag—as Mr. Meade had taught us it was—was the very thing that sent many of our ancestors into a war about which they did not care and from which they would not benefit since they were too poor to be affected by slavery one way or the other.

Still, though, so many poor white Southerners clung to that flag and all the hate it stood for because hate was about the only thing that felt like it was going to get them anywhere. They were wrong, of course, and dangerous in their anger. But I understood why they felt it, even if I wished they could see how much we could all gain if we fought the problems together instead of in these factions.

Mayor Tucker had come back across the road to join us, and he took Shamila's hand. I saw his father across the street, a scowl set deep into his cheeks, and I said quietly, "It's like the Civil War all over again, son set against father." I was feeling a little melodramatic.

Beatrice pointed up the street at her news van and then squeezed my hand before she let go and headed over. Isaiah slid over to fill her spot, and I held his hand tight.

We stood that way for a long time, quiet and staring at one another, but then, someone started to sing. I knew that people used to sing "We Shall Overcome" and "Kumbayah" at the Civil Rights marches, but we were mountain people. Slowly, the air started to fill with "I'll Fly Away." It was a hymn that most everybody knew from church, and if they didn't, it was simple enough to pick up quickly.

I'll fly away, oh glory.
I'll fly away.
When I die, hallelujah by and by,
I'll fly away.

I thought of the memorial service for Bo and the choir's song, and then I thought of Sarah, . . . and I wished she could be here to see people lined up to honor her mama, even if they didn't know it.

Soon, several more news vans showed up, even a couple from Charlottesville and one from Roanoke. I could see Beatrice coordinating all the reporters, handing them fact-sheets that she'd gotten the library to print out for her, pointing them to the best vantage points for good camera angles. I even saw a helicopter fly over as we stood and sang through songs ranging from "Amazing Grace" to "All Along the Watchtower." I was suddenly very grateful for Mom's Bob Dylan collection.

I guess I started to get complacent as we sang because I was totally surprised when I saw a group of men adjust their guns and head across the street toward us. Virginia is an open carry state, so it's possible to walk around with your loaded gun on you at any time as long as everybody can see it. Sadly, every other teenager in the U.S. and I had become far too familiar with gun law in the past couple of years. So I wasn't surprised by the guns. Disconcerted, yes. Surprised, no. But to see armed men actually coming closer to me, that caught me off guard. I guess I'd thought they would eventually give up whatever they were trying to do—scare me to death, I imagined—and go home. But no, now they were marching at me, and my heart felt like it would beat out of my chest.

Most of the men coming our way were in what Isaiah would call "business casual" attire. Khakis and polo shirts. A couple had on the more stereotypical combat boots, camo, and American flag T-shirts, but the others looked like they had walked out of the office buildings nearby on lunch break, . . . and they probably had. Johnny Tucker, walker moving ahead of him at a good clip, was leading the charge.

I could see Stephen Douglas on the steps of the coffee shop behind us. A group of police officers was gathered around him, and as they noticed the men coming over, they moved towards us. We had let Stephen know we didn't want one of those photo ops where police in riot gear stood off against protestors, but we also had said we would appreciate their presence, just in case. As I caught Stephen's eye, he tossed his head up the street, and I could see the lights of several police cars and the tactical unit trailer parked at the next intersection.

The men from across the road—everyone one of them white —stopped right in front us, their noses just inches from ours. Well, except for Johnny Tucker. He was just as close, but his stooped body made him square off with my breasts. It would have been funny and awkward if I wasn't so damn scared.

Javier squeezed my hand, and I took a deep breath. "You're not scaring me away, Mr. Tucker."

"I wish you'd be scared, girl. Being afraid now could save you a lot of pain later."

"What does that mean, sir?" I was following all the advice I'd ever heard about deescalating a situation: speak evenly; keep a calm demeanor; be clear.

"It means, Ms. Steele, that things are going to get a whole lot worse for you"—he looked up and down the line—"and for your friends if you don't back off on this whole Jennings thing."

"I want to be sure I understand." I leaned over so I could look him in the eye, and I was close enough to smell his after-shave. "Are you threatening me?"

"Oh girl, I don't threaten. I just follow through."

I heard the unmistakable sound of a shell being chambered into a shotgun and stood up straight. Then, I looked over my shoulder to Beatrice, who had come up behind me as the men approached. "Did you get all that, Beatrice?"

"Every word. Live." She held up her microphone.

If I had expecting Johnny Tucker to look embarrassed or to back off, I would have been surprised when he stepped forward and took the microphone off Beatrice's lapel with a hard tug. But you don't carefully plan a public action on Main Street in broad daylight in any town if you don't think you're willing to go pretty far with things, so while I was very unhappy that he laid hands on my friend—Stephen stepped up really quickly then—I wasn't surprised.

"This still live, girl?" he said to Beatrice. She raised one eyebrow and then nodded.

"Listen here. We aren't backing down. This girl, Mary Steele, and her friends are nosing about in business that isn't theirs. They're doing that thing all these 'black lives matter' people do and bringing up stuff from so long ago that almost nobody remembers it. It's time to let the past go. We've moved on. Everybody has equal opportunities now, even ni—even African Americans." The sneer in his voice was audible. "So we'll stand here and protest, we'll take action, we'll make this stop if people don't stop on their own. If you'd like to join us, we meet tonight—"

I saw Beatrice slice her flat hand across her throat, and her cameraman instantly dropped his camera and flicked a switch.

"You can't do that. I have as much a right to free speech as anyone else." Johnny Tucker's face was as red as a poppy bloom. "Turn it back on."

Beatrice jerked her microphone from his hand and said, "You had your say, Mr. Tucker. But we don't do advertisements for any group, and we especially don't do them for hate groups." She turned and walked back to her station's van on the corner.

"Don't worry, Johnny," a man in a white button-down shirt and blue dress pants said. "I put it out live on Facebook and YouTube with the address and time. It's getting shared like crazy."

Out of the corner of my eye, I could see Stephen typing quickly on his phone. Locating and then texting the address to his station, I expected.

While Stephen and the other officers were distracted with what was happening tonight, Johnny Tucker leaned in close, his head turned up to my chin. "Everyone at that meeting tonight will know your address, little girl. You think a little burning carpet was bad—"

Mayor Tucker came over quickly and jerked his father by the arm, hard. "Dad, you are out of line. One more word, and I'll have you arrested."

"You can't do that. You're not the mayor here."

"No, I'm not, but I heard you make a threat to Mary here, and that's intimidation. That's a crime. Either you and your friends here leave this street immediately, or I'll have you arrested while all of these cameras roll."

"You wouldn't do that to me. I'm your father."

"You are my father, and it would break my heart. But I would do it because this kind of hatred, it's already eaten your soul. I won't let it destroy anyone else."

"This is bigger than me, son. You know that. I'm leaving, but don't you dare think"—he looked me dead in the eye—"this is over."

17

*S*oon after Johnny Tucker's departure in his convoy of Confederate-clad vehicles, the crowd had begun to thin, the bicyclists were headed back home, and my energy was waning. I felt like I could sleep for days, but I didn't have that luxury. Tomorrow was the Jennings's Family Reunion, and I had a buttload of potato salad to make.

We knew that Johnny Tucker's rally was happening at the old high school football stadium downtown that night, but Stephen told us it was best if we didn't show up, and he didn't get even a second of argument from me. I knew we'd hear about it on the news anyway.

After picking up twenty pounds of potatoes, a jar of mayo as big as my head, and one of those giant jars of parsley flakes, everyone headed back to the safe house. Stephen had agreed to share the address with my group of friends because he figured we needed to all be together tonight, but he made all of us swear on our smartphones that we wouldn't tell a soul the address. Of course, everyone swore. But of course, no one had needed to. We had been through too much to betray each other now.

Carrying the groceries in, I felt like a herd of hippos had charged over my body. I just wanted to turn on the TV, pull a blanket way up to my chin, and pretend the real world included mutants who could shoot sunlight out of their hands. But, like I said, potato salad.

Mom, Marcie, Isaiah, and I cut potatoes into cubes while Javier and Nicole boiled water and cooked then drained the spuds in every pot we had in the house. Beatrice had gone back to the station to prepare her story for the evening news, and Shamila and Mr. Meade had stayed in Lexington to pick up an order of the best Indian food around because we needed it. Samosas are my heart's true joy.

Everyone tried to make light-hearted conversation about the reunion: What should we wear? Did we all own elastic-waisted pants? How many helpings is considered rude? But eventually, it got very quiet in the kitchen.

We were on the last round potatoes when Javier dropped a pot right in the middle of the kitchen. "Damn it!" he shouted, and then quickly, "I'm sorry, Mrs. Steele."

"Don't worry about it, Javier. You didn't burn yourself, did you?"

"No, ma'am. I'm fine." His voice was shaky. He bent down to scoop the potatoes back into the pot, but Mom stopped him.

"I've got this." She looked over at me. "Why don't you and Mary take a break? We're almost done."

I didn't know what was going on with Javier, but I was all for a break from all the steam and the stirring of mayo and parsley in big bowls. We headed toward the living room, and that's when I finally noticed. Javier was crying.

I pulled him close, and as he sobbed against me, I waddled us over to the couch and hugged him down. I'd had so many moments like this with Javier, except this was the first time that I was the one holding him. I knew, though, that what I had always needed was to just get it all out, so I just sat there with my arms around him as he soaked my shirt through.

In a few minutes, his breathing eased, and he sat up and

looked away, out the window. "I'm sorry." His voice was almost a whisper.

"Stop that. You have nothing to be sorry for." I was amazed at how much I sounded like my mother, but that didn't stop me. "It's been a brutal day. A brutal year. And you have always been the strong one. It was my turn."

He looked at me out of the corner of his eye. "Well, thanks."

"Do you want to talk about it?"

"Nah. I'll be okay. I mean, this is all just so much, right? And then they're threatening you, and I can't do anything. And I can't really sleep on the floor of your room." He looked up at me. "I can't, right?"

"Right."

"And you're having to live in this crappy safe house, and I keep finding out that more and more people hate black and brown people. And"—he took a deep breath—"I really hate cooking potatoes." He gave me a small smile.

"Me too. But the good news is, the potatoes are cooked, . . . and I think—although I can make no promises—that the worst of the trouble will be over tomorrow."

"Really?!" The hope in his voice rang through the air.

"I think so."

"How do you know?"

"Well, I don't know, but there's some feeling I have, something seems to be working itself out." I shook my head. "I can't really explain it."

"That's okay. I feel better knowing this whole mess might be done soon."

I gave him a big smile.

He gave me a quick kiss. "I guess we better get back in there and help, huh?"

"Yep. I just need to go to the bathroom. Be right behind you."

I held it together until I closed the door to the dingy safe house bathroom. Then, I broke down and sobbed while I let the water run in the sink.

I really did think all this tension caused by the fact that I could see Sarah would be over tomorrow, but apparently, I was going to be doing this for the rest of my life. I guess I'd just have to get used to it . . . and get good at crying in bathrooms.

By the time I emerged, the potato salad was done and packed into every Tupperware and bowl that the safe house had to offer. Now, the real work began.

Stephen, Shamila, and Mr. Meade had come in while I was in the bathroom. It was almost eight o'clock, and Johnny Tucker's rally had turned out to be a dud. Just a few dozen guys in pickup trucks with make-shift tiki torches wandering around the field. They were gathered without a permit, and it hadn't taken long to break up the "rally."

As Stephen said, "A little more notice—like they'd had in Charlottesville—and things could have been ugly. But trying to get even white supremacists to break their plans for a Saturday night on the spur of the moment . . ."

A tired chuckle passed around the room.

When I walked into the kitchen, I gasped at the wide array of food, but my scan didn't reveal any samosas. I thought I might cry again until I noticed the crooked grin on Javier's face and watched him slide a whole platter of that potato-ey goodness from behind the microwave. "You stinker!" I shouted, and he grinned wider.

It felt so natural for all of us to find seats wherever there was space and eat off our laps while we planned yet another gathering that would garner us hatred and put people in danger. Someday, I hoped we would all get together to celebrate a birthday or even just to watch the Super Bowl, not take on racism.

Within a few minutes, we had a plan for the next day. Stephen would have a contingent of plainclothes police officers at the reunion. They'd hang back for the most part, but should something start up, they'd be on hand. "We will also have the tactical unit available just down the road. It took them a few minutes to get there today. Tomorrow, they can be there in seconds."

"I wish I thought that was overkill," Isaiah said. I knew just what he meant.

Beatrice said, "The news station will be there to film a segment, too, and we'll be ready to go live if need be." She shoveled in a big mouthful of biryani. For a tiny woman, that girl could eat.

The rest of the conversation centered around who was bringing what and when. Mom, Isaiah, and I planned to head into Terra Linda early for church before heading to the reunion. Javier and his friends had borrowed some tents from the local funeral home—it was a pretty standard thing to use funeral tents for events around us, free advertising for them and rain protection for us—so they'd get those set up before everyone else arrived around noon to set up tables and hang balloons and such.

My only other job was to go see Sarah before the gathering started. We knew she couldn't be there—being tethered to a place and all—but I didn't want to leave her out entirely. She was, after all, the reason we were gathering.

The next morning, as soon as the first service at church was over, we headed to the lock to see Sarah. She was there, same as always, but this time, she was bouncing, so excited that she could barely stand still.

I had barely stepped out of the car when she said, "Watch this," and off she headed into the river and stepped onto the opposite shore.

I was confused, but she quickly ran back and said, "I've never been able to do that before."

As she ran away again—this time up 60 toward the Coffee Pot—I finally figured out what was going on and felt a river of hope rush through me.

When she jogged back over, I grabbed her by the arm and pulled her to the picnic table. "You're untethered."

She nodded and started to run off again, but I tugged her down to sit beside me.

"How did this happen?" I had never—not in my limited but deep experience with ghosts—seen one not bound to a place. Melinda Gordon and I disagreed about this; I knew that places were haunted, not people.

"I have no idea. All this time, I had only thought to walk as far as that rock, the lock, and the road." She pointed around at the narrow circle of land. "I somehow just knew I couldn't go any farther, and to be honest, it hadn't really bothered me. Just like it hadn't bothered me that I had been here, what, ninety years, until you came and could see me. Suddenly, then, time seemed much more relevant. It was the same with place. This morning, I just felt like I wanted to see what was up on that hill over there." She pointed across the river. "So I went to see, and as I stepped out of the river on the other side and looked back at that tree, I realized what had happened."

She stared up at the sycamore where they had murdered her mother. "Now, I can't wait to get away from here. I only stayed this long so I could tell you."

"Well, I'm glad you did. I would have been sad and missed you if you'd just left."

"Oh, I didn't think of that." She studied her hands. "I just figured you'd think I'd crossed over or something, and I didn't want to scare you if I showed up a few years from now to say hi."

I smiled. "I could never be scared of you, Sarah." She looked up at me then, and I saw a tear on her cheek. "But this news couldn't come at a better time. The Jennings family reunion is this afternoon. I was just coming by to catch you up on things and tell you the plan for the afternoon, but now, now you can come."

If a smile could cast shadows, hers would have. "I can? I can see my grandchildren."

"Yep." I let out a shuddery breath so I wouldn't cry. "Let's go."

As we walked to the car, Sarah looked up at the hill across the river.

"Whatcha looking at?" She was obviously seeing something.

"An old cemetery. I wouldn't have known it was one if it wasn't for the way them old stones was laid out in neat rows. It was peaceful."

Sarah slid into the seat beside Mom, and I closed her door, staring up at the hill until Mom beeped the horn and made me get in the car.

I didn't have much time to think about the cemetery, although I knew from past experience that any cemetery that wasn't marked was probably pretty important, as we drove to Wildy Holler, where Sarah's family had lived. Sarah was busy telling Mom about her untethering, and Mom kept asking me questions about how that could happen as if I were some sort of ghost expert. She finally quit pushing me when I snapped, "Do I look like I have an EVP recorder or something?"

Still, the question did puzzle me. What exactly would free someone from the place they had haunted for ninety years?

When we reached the reunion, I got my answer, and it wasn't one I expected. As Sarah climbed out of the car, Mrs. Garrison came over, hugged her, and exclaimed, "It worked!"

I looked back and forth between mother and daughter. They resembled each other so strongly that I almost missed what Mrs. Garrison said. Almost. "What worked?"

"Oh, my severing prayer."

"You prayed that Sarah would be untethered?"

"No, child. I prayed that she could come to the reunion. And it took a severing to make that happen."

Sarah hugged her daughter again. "Thank you, Jo."

"But look here. Don't touch her now." Mrs. Garrison gave me a stern look. "We don't need anyone having a heart attack from fright."

I grinned. "Yes, ma'am." I nodded but then looked back to Mrs. Garrison. "So wait, when you touch a ghost, it doesn't make them visible to the other people who are there?"

"No, ma'am. It does not. That's your thing."

I let out a long low breath.

As the two women wrapped arms around each other's waists, I looked around to see the tents, the food tables, and the DJ talking with Isaiah. I looked at his equipment and then at Mrs. Garrison.

"It's not a party without some tunes." She shook her hips a little bit and made duck lips.

I cracked up and bent double with laughter.

"What, you thought an old lady couldn't appreciate Queen Bey?"

"Alright now," Marcie said as she gave Mrs. Garrison a high five. It was going to be a good day.

And it was. So many members of the Jennings family came; Mom counted over 120. We ate. We laughed. We talked.

I ate five kinds of macaroni and cheese and only stopped because I could feel my stomach against my rib cage. Mrs. Garrison gave a little speech about the value of family and invited the mayor to share the stage with her again. Then, she called Shamila up, and Nicole, Marcie, and I distributed booklets of the Jennings family history that the historical society had created for them. Shamila walked them through their family line all the way back to 1870—she couldn't get past the census for that year, she'd said. But she told everyone she'd love to hear family stories and see if the family history couldn't be taken back a few generations.

When she was done, the family gave her a standing ovation, and I saw several people head for her table, where she'd set up her laptop, a notebook, and a pen. I figured they'd have the family line traced back to Adam in about forty-five minutes.

Sarah looked to be enjoying the day too. For the most part, she sat at a corner table where I had set my backpack in a chair.

She basically sat through the backpack, but it kept anyone from sitting in her, which would have been even more awkward and weird. I kept checking in on her, and she just kept saying, "I have so many people." The babies seemed to capture her attention most. Each time one would pass by in the arms of an auntie or uncle, she'd grin.

I so wished she could hold them all.

The day had settled into what Isaiah called, "The good part," where all the planned things had been done, and now we were all just enjoying each other. The sun was out and the day warmer than usual for that time of year, and folks had circled up together to share stories and jabs, make jokes and talk about plans.

I was keeping busy by picking up loose trash and matching container lids to bottoms when I heard them coming—roaring engines.

I knew who it was immediately, and so did everyone else, it appeared, because in the flash of an eye, everyone who could stand was on their feet. Several men and a couple of women had moved toward cars, and I saw cellphone cameras come out and up to the ready.

In that instant before it all broke loose, I thought, *Black people are always at the ready for violence against them.* That idea would have made me still with sorrow if I didn't know I needed to get ready myself. I dug my phone out of my back pocket, put it in front of me, and hit "Live Video" on Facebook as the first pickup rolled into sight.

Truck after truck pulled up the road and off into the grass by the reunion. Soon, the street was lined with pickups and a few cars. Most of the people in the neighboring houses had come out, taken a look at the situation, and gone inside. I could see a few faces at windows, often with cameras, but not a few of the windows were quickly blocked with curtains or blinds. I couldn't blame them. I didn't want to be here, and I was white, unlike most of the residents in this little community.

Mayor Tucker approached his father as Johnny Tucker was

helped down from the lead pickup. "Dad, what are you doing? This is a private gathering."

"That's not what I heard. I heard it's a family reunion for all the Jennings kin, which means I'm invited. I thought you'd be happy to see me since you've been making such a stink about this whole mess." The snide grin on Johnny Tucker's face made me wince.

"Well, then, let me introduce you to the family." The mayor took his father's walker from a man in a red baseball cap and steered his father toward the gathering. Mrs. Garrison gave me a nod and headed his way. I followed with Sarah close behind.

"Mr. Tucker, or should I say, Cousin"—now it was Johnny Tucker's turn to wince—"I'm so glad you could make it. Mind if I introduce you to everyone." Mrs. Garrison's voice was cool and clear.

"In fact, I do mind—"

But Mrs. Garrison carried right along as if she hadn't heard him, winking at me as she led the way into the gathering of tables. She began to introduce Johnny Tucker to everyone, even the babies, by first name and family relation always calling him "Cousin Johnny" because he was, in fact, her uncle.

I stayed close by Mrs. Garrison, and I noticed Stephen was nearby too. But each time I looked over at the group of men gathered by the pickups, I got chills. They had their guns resting across their chests, and many of them were carrying Confederate flags or wearing Confederate T-shirts. Part of me was just glad they didn't have last night's tiki torches.

I could also see that the plain-clothed police officers had gathered between the Jennings family and the men although I wasn't sure the white supremacists knew they were officers. Most of the men were black volunteers who had come so that they could blend in more and disrupt the reunion less. Still, I knew they each had a concealed weapon and more firepower in their cars that were parked at the back of the lot.

When the introductions were done, Mrs. Garrison said, "I'm

afraid you missed the meal, Cousin, but I'm sure we could scrounge you up some banana pudding if you'd like." They had moved off to a table at the edge of the lot, away from everyone else.

"That's enough." His face was bright red. "I was trying to be polite while all you nig—, you people ogled me, but I am NOT your cousin. I don't care what you say. And we are here because enough is enough. You need to stop this nonsense"—he turned to look at me—"of making a spectacle of ancient history. And if you won't stop voluntarily, we're prepared to make you stop."

He was shouting now, so the crowd heard him. And in the silence following his proclamation, I heard the quiet sound of cloth rustling. When I glanced behind me, I saw rifles, shotguns, and a fair number of pistols in the hands of the Jennings family members. Mrs. Garrison wasn't bluffing about white people not being the only ones packing.

Stephen moved quickly to my side. "That'll be all today, Johnny. One more word, and I'll arrest you for intimidation."

"Arrest me then because unless I get this girl's word"—he jabbed me in the chest with his finger—"on the record that she's going to stop talking about and looking into the death of Beverly Jennings, we're going to end this here today OUR way." He looked at Beatrice and her cameraman, who had been rolling the whole time. But to Beatrice's credit, neither she nor the cameraman moved their focus off Johnny Tucker.

Mom moved quickly to my side as Stephen Douglas turned Johnny Tucker around and put him in handcuffs.

Beyond them, I could see the white supremacists chambering shots in their long guns and pulling back hammers on their pistols.

I was about to be in the middle of a shoot-out.

Mayor Tucker stepped into the open space between the Jennings and Johnny Tucker's crew and raised his hands in the air. "Now, before this gets out of hand, let's all talk about this."

Mrs. Garrison stepped up to the mayor and whispered in his

ear. He gave her a puzzled look and then stepped back to stand beside Mom and me. When I glanced over, I could see that Javier, Marcie, and the rest of our friends had lined up beside me too.

Then, Mrs. Garrison spoke. "Gentlemen, thank you for coming to our reunion. We are fixing to pack up for the day, and unless you'd like to be recruited to fold up chairs and wash dishes"—she gestured toward the galvanized tubs of soapy water near the road—"I reckon you might want to be heading on home to your families."

The men didn't look one bit like they were going to be heading home, but then, I saw what they hadn't yet noticed: the people from the houses around us had come out into their yards, and all of them were armed. Some of them had guns and some cellphone cameras, but if those men opened fire, every angle of their action was going to be sent out live into the world. No court, even in our racist little community, would be able to let them go on this one.

"Gentlemen, we'll thank you to be moving along." Mrs. Garrison gestured behind the men, and as they realized they were not only outnumbered but outranked in firepower, they began to head slowly to their cars.

The day ended uneventfully with the loading of tables and tents onto trucks and the pawning off or hoarding of potluck leftovers. But even though the excitement had calmed down, we were all still keyed up. I could see it in the way everyone's eyes kept darting toward the road to see if those trucks were coming back.

Stephen and his fellow officers stayed on hand, and I noticed a few of the Jennings men lingered until we were all in our cars. It was nice to have people looking out for one another, . . . especially when it was obvious someone had ideas other than being neighborly.

Part of me really hoped everyone would come back to the safe house, drink hot cocoa, and watch some Hallmark ridiculousness, but the other part of me just wanted my mom. It turned out that my mom knew best and told everyone I'd see them tomorrow before ushering me to the car and kissing Isaiah goodbye. I waved to Sarah, who had told me that Marcie was going to give her a ride back to the lock. I had told her she was welcome to come with us, but she said she'd just as soon go back. She'd had enough excitement for the day.

Mom and I hadn't even gotten down the lane out of the hollow when I started to shake. She reached over and put a hand on my leg as I let my body be wracked by the fear and sorrow I had been carrying since those trucks had pulled up. Years of work as a therapist had taught Mom that the best thing for someone moving through intense emotion was presence, not words—she'd shared that lesson with me many times—so she just rubbed my leg as she drove us to the safe house. By the time we arrived, I was able to breath more easily, even though it felt like someone had filled my head with Styrofoam.

She sent me to "my" bedroom and told me to put on pj's. Then, we sat on the couch and watched a movie where a woman gives up her career as a Hollywood producer to begin her dream of running a vinegar shop in some New Hampshire town. It was perfect. . . . Not that I actually watched it. I fell asleep almost as soon as the boy met the girl.

I woke up a couple of hours later from a dream about a cemetery where all the tombstones could talk but I couldn't understand them. Frustration lingered in my body as I tried to figure out where I was.

Mom was asleep next to me on the couch, her head tilted back and her mouth wide open "catching flies" as Mrs. Garrison would have said. When I stood to lay my blanket over her, she stirred and opened her eyes. "Movie over?" she asked groggily.

I glanced at the TV and saw an infomercial for some sort of special frying pan that could cook an egg in 3.2 seconds. "Long over." I smiled.

"Want to talk?" She stretched and turned her body toward

the center of the sofa. I was so exhausted, but I was also wide awake. My dream had reminded me of what Sarah had said about the cemetery on the hill, and it didn't take a degree in psychology to interpret what the tombstones had wanted to tell me.

"I need to go to the lock."

"Okay, after school tomorrow, I'll take you."

"No, I need to go now." I surprised myself with the urgency I felt, but now that I'd said I needed to go, it felt like I might just materialize there myself if Mom didn't agree to take me, and right this minute. I had never felt like that before, like I could predict when I would do my magically-materializing thing. But I knew that if I didn't hold myself back, that's exactly what I was going to do. And I didn't know how long I could hold myself back.

Mom looked at me closely and stood up. "Get your jacket." She slung her long wool coat over her shoulders and grabbed her purse. I followed close behind, my hot-pink pajamas sticking out beneath my puffy blue jacket. This time, though, I made sure I put on shoes.

Part of me wanted to text everyone on our way over, but somehow, I knew I needed to do this on my own . . . or as much on my own as Mom was going to let me. So I stared at the window as Mom made her way down to 60 and over the hill.

I saw Sarah as soon as we arrived. She was looking across the river to the top of the hill, and she was smiling. I got out of the car and walked over to her, following her gaze with my own. There, at the top of the hill, was Bo Jennings, Sarah's mother, looking as alive as she could be. Or at least more alive than she had looked when I had cut her ghostly body down from the tree. She was smiling down at Sarah and me and waving us over, across the river.

I glanced at Sarah. "I was waiting for you," she said.

I looked down at the water, at my Converse high tops, and then up at Mom. I could not possibly walk across this river, not on an April night, not on any night. I had no idea how strong the current was anyway. I could be the next ghost at the lock if I weren't careful.

I had just turned to tell Mom what was happening when I felt it—a tug. Not even a strong tug. Just the kind of pull you might feel if you stepped into a spider web and broke it with your face. But I knew, instantly, what it was, and as I let it take me, I held one finger up to Mom to say, *I'll be right back.*

Then, I found myself over on the top of the hill with Bo Jennings and Sarah too. Down below, I could see Mom; she looked completely bewildered. She kept spinning in circles as if she were suddenly going to find me standing there. I whistled to her—a whistle she'd taught me in case I might need help in a crowd someday—and she turned quickly toward me. I waved, and she waved back slowly. I made the one-finger-pointing-up gesture again. She nodded and headed toward her car to wait for me.

I turned to Sarah, and she was grinning. "Mary, this is my mom. Mama, this is Mary."

"Pleasure, Mary. I owe you my gratitude for helping my girl send me on my way, here."

I looked at Ms. Jennings closely. Her skin was flawless and her face round, open, friendly. "I apologize. I'm not sure what you mean, ma'am."

"Why, child, you cut my body down, helped my Sarah do what she been wanting to do a long time."

"Um, well, you're welcome. Yes, I did do that, I guess."

Sarah was staring at her mother, and I realized that I was in the middle of a reunion that had been ninety years in the making. I thought the two of them may appreciate some time to themselves. "If you'll excuse me a moment, I'd like to see that cemetery you told me about, Sarah." I took a few steps back and then turned around.

I walked a bit farther into the trees ahead of me and surveyed the ground. Mostly, all I could see by the faint moonlight were leaves, but as I crunched through them, I felt my toe butt up against something firm. I bent down and gently pushed back the leaves—it was a small stone about the size of a softball. I kept walking; every few steps I came upon another stone. Within a few minutes, I'd uncovered half a dozen stones, all placed about six or eight feet apart. The cemetery Sarah had mentioned.

A bit later, Sarah and Bo walked over to me and looked at the stones, veins of something silver shining in the moonlight.

"That there, that's Davy Willis." Bo said, pointing toward the stone closest to me. "And that one's Minerva Case. Jauncy Ferguson and Scotty Bruce are over there. Them's Marcus and Scipio Jones, brothers hanged for stealing a horse when Scipio's wife needed a doctor."

I stared at the stones, carefully chosen markers for the graves of people Bo Jennings clearly knew.

"You knew all these people?"

"Oh no, child. I just know their names and places. Mama made sure of that. She didn't want me to forget." She walked a few feet away and uncovered another stone. "This one here is mine. Joshua laid it for me after he cut my body down from that tree."

I looked up from the stone and looked at her face. "This is where you are buried."

She stared down at her grave marker. "Yes, ma'am, it is. Best view in the county, I say."

I walked back over to the bluff overlooking the river and found myself agreeing. The gentle bend of the Maury and the way the hills ahead sloped up and above, it was peaceful as any place I'd ever been. I found that cemeteries usually were.

"But why here?" Sarah asked. She was holding her mother's hand and spoke in a hushed voice.

Bo looked up and turned to her daughter. "Because this, my girl, is where they buried us folks who was lynched. Been the place since my granddaddy was a boy."

I felt my eyes grow big. "How many people are buried here,

Bo?" I couldn't see any edge to the cemetery. It was just here, amongst the trees.

"Twenty-nine. Twenty-nine of us resting here. Grandaddy and his brothers chose this place when their cousin Julius got killed by a bunch of white boys who said he got one of their wives pregnant. Wouldn't you know that baby was as white as the driven snow, but no one felt any sort of bad about it. Not the white folks anyway. His grave's that one, the one with the big white stone on it."

I could just make out the shimmer of a white rock about twenty feet away.

"Twenty-nine people were lynched here? In Terra Linda?"

"That's right. Here or near abouts. Grandaddy chose this place because it was secluded and quiet, figured nobody'd mess with graves this far out. Plus, it was close to the lynching tree. Easy to carry bodies up at night."

I blinked my eyes several times, trying to make sense of what she had said. "Wait. Let me see if I understand." I walked back over to the bluff and pointed. "That tree. The one, forgive me, they hanged you on." She gave me a wan smile. "They hanged other people there too?"

"They did. Not all these folks, mind you. Some of them was hanged on the first lynching tree. Some said it got chopped down, but it actually fell over in a storm. So they had to use this new tree."

I could see the white bark of the sycamore from where I stood. To think that tree had been forced to do that work not just once but over and over, . . . and that before that tree, another tree had been put to the same horrible labor. The lives taken on that land. It's a wonder only Sarah haunted it.

Bo looked at me. "When they came and got me, I knowed this was where I was going."

Sarah whipped her head around to her mother. "You knew?"

"Yes, dear. Everybody knowed."

"I didn't." Sarah's voice was hot with anger.

"That was on purpose. I didn't want you to know about this. I hoped you'd never have to know." She put her hand on her daughter's face. "I was protecting you." She took a shuddering breath. "Some lot of good that did."

Sarah's face softened. "You raised me good, Mama. But I wish you'd told me."

"I knowed soon as I saw Gilford Tucker, just as soon as he and those other two boys rode into the yard. They didn't come for no house call."

Sudden as a flash, I realized that it was this—this cemetery, these people, this information Bo was giving me—that Johnny Tucker was trying to scare us off from finding. He didn't want people to know that not only did his father kill two people: Bo and Sarah, but that he was responsible for running Terra Linda's lynch mob. He was a serial killer, and Johnny Tucker was terrified people would find out.

I had to tell Mom. I had to tell everyone because I knew that once we told people about the cemetery, about the regular use of the land by the lock as a lynching ground, Sarah would be freed and so would Bo.

And just like that, I was back by the lock, and Mom was stepping out of the car with a look of awe on her face. "You can control it now?"

"A little bit, I guess. But Mom, you won't believe . . ."

By the time I got to lunch on Monday, I was practically mobbed with questions about the cemetery and the rumors of multiple lynchings at the lock. People who never gave me a second thought were suddenly bombarding me with questions. This was the new big news, and I was the one in the know.

At another point, even just a few months earlier, I might have craved all the attention, but now, after all the events of the past year, I just wanted to eat my two slices of pepperoni and drink my chocolate milk in peace.

Fortunately, Mr. Meade saved me by having me paged to his

classroom, and I dodged the questioners as I bolted from the lunchroom.

When I'd texted Beatrice that morning, she'd come right over and interviewed me as I brushed my teeth. This was a huge find, and she wanted it on the early show. . . . Shamila had done a blast email to the historical society newsletter, and somehow, Nicole had even gotten a blip about the story onto Channel One so that everyone in the school saw it in homeroom. I was more famous than I'd ever wanted to be, and while I was actually happy that the people buried in the cemetery were going to be remembered, I just wished I'd been able to stay out of the story.

Mr. Meade had paged me because a reporter from *Good Morning America* had contacted him through the school and wanted to interview me during seventh period. She was flying down from New York as we spoke, and Mr. Meade knew that I would say yes but that I would also need some time to think about what I wanted to say. Mom had been notified, of course, and she'd come over to the school and met me in Mr. Meade's classroom. Now, Mom and I were brainstorming answers to questions the reporter might ask while Javier ran to our house and got everything out of my closet. Beatrice had texted me to say, "No white. No stripes. No super loud colors." I had no idea what that meant, so Javier was bringing everything. When Mom asked him for the favor his shoulders drooped, but once he saw the look of panic on my face, he knew I needed my mom and went without complaint after squeezing my hand.

The reporter wanted to interview Mrs. Garrison and me—Mr. Meade had let the reporter know about that Bo Jennings had a living daughter—at the lock at two p.m. I had less than two hours to prepare, and it felt like two years wouldn't even be enough. I kept imagining myself needing to breath into a paper bag just to be able to get through the interview.

Then, an image of Johnny Tucker leaning into my face over his walker flashed into my mind, and I had to catch myself on Mr. Meade's desk.

"Mary, sit down," he said and rolled his chair over. "What happened?"

"Who else knows about the interview?" My eyes darted from him, to Mom, and back to him again.

"Just us. No one else." He looked directly into my eyes. "And we made sure no one told anyone. We even asked Mrs. Garrison to keep the news to herself until after the interview was over."

Mom pulled a student desk over and sat down directly in front of me. "Not even the mayor knows, Mary. Johnny Tucker and his friends will not find out."

"Plus, we'll be there, Mary." Blanch stood at the doorway. His bodyguard duties had continued after the bathroom incident, but now, the police had also assigned a fully-trained officer at the school to keep an eye on things. I was always glad to see Blanch in the halls, but today, I felt a particularly strong wave of relief wash over me. "Stephen will be there, too, with a few other officers. We're bringing a van so there won't be too many cars at the lock wayside."

As everyone explained to me how they had done everything they could to keep me safe, I felt myself relax a bit . . . until I remembered I was going to be on national TV, that Carson Daly might say my name, and then I began to stress out again.

Mom and I nailed down some basic statements for the interview: the location of the graveyard, how I'd found it when I was wandering the hill above the lock over the weekend, how Shamila had helped me research lynchings on a hunch about the odd location of the cemetery, and how we'd confirmed the nature of the cemetery by interviewing an old man—who preferred to remain anonymous—who remembered helping his father bury a young man's body there after the man was hanged by the lock. That last part was entirely fictional, but we all knew I couldn't tell everyone the ghosts of Bo and Sarah Jennings had told me. We knew we were telling the truth about the cemetery itself, so it didn't really matter how we came to know it—at least not enough to subject me to the potential danger, awful scrutiny, and potential ridicule that revealing my abilities on national television would bring.

I picked out a red blouse and long black skirt that I had worn in last year's choir concert, and Marcie helped me put my hair in some semblance of a style with a few bobby pins Mom had found in her purse.

Mrs. Garrison joined us in the classroom, and her lavender suit was the perfect blend of professional and fun, just like her. She had on the most adorable white tennis shoes, and she was carrying a white cane. I asked her about it since I hadn't seen it before. "People expect old ladies to have canes, but they don't expect that I can take them down at the knees with this thing. I carry it as protection, not a walking aid, girl." She grinned at me, and I laughed out loud as I gave her a little punch on the arm. This woman was a trip.

We had just begun to gather our things to head for the church vans Isaiah had arranged for us to borrow when the lockdown alarms went off. I knew what they were because the previous year, a couple of guys who were running drugs up to New York via I-81 had taken the police on a car chase that ended up in our school parking lot and put us all on lockdown for three hours. But this time, I knew as soon as I heard them that this wasn't a random incident. A loud click on the classroom door told us we'd been locked in the room, and within a minute or two, the principal's voice came over the loudspeakers to tell us we were in lockdown because several armed men had arrived at the school and had taken a classroom of students hostage.

It took only seconds for Marcie to figure out that it was Mrs. Keene's Spanish class in the room closest to the front stairwell that was being held hostage, and soon, we could all see photos surreptitiously snapped and being sent via Snapchat. Four men, all with what looked like machine guns were in the room. The guns were terrifying, but the men actually looked as scared as the kids they were holding hostage.

Then, a student posted a video to Facebook. It showed

Johnny Tucker and a lineup of trucks in the bus lane in front of the school. Mr. Tucker had made bail almost as soon as they'd put him in the county jail—Stephen had let us know that right away just in case—and now, he looked madder than ever.

In the video, Johnny had a megaphone, and he was demanding that every news station in the area send a reporter. "I want everyone to see this. Everyone needs to know what this girl, Mary Steele, is trying to do." He said he'd make his demands once the news vans arrived, but if anyone tried anything, his men on the inside—"I don't want to do this," he said—would show everyone how serious they were about their mission.

He sounded absolutely insane, and I was sure that's what people would say, particularly those people who wanted to make school shootings about only mental health rather than reasonable gun laws. But I knew he wasn't insane. He was just furious. Furious and scared.

For some reason I didn't understand, I suddenly became very calm as the sirens outside grew louder and more numerous and the announcements to remain calm sounded less and less so. I was worried about the kids in that classroom, and I was worried about us. But I knew, somehow, that in the end, Johnny Tucker was just a really sad, scared man who was acting out like a child, . . . and I knew it would be okay. I have no explanation other than that "peace that passes understanding" people talk about. But there it was.

After a few minutes of mild panic, everyone else in Mr. Meade's room began to calm down, too, and then we did what we do best: we began to plan. Blanch was in touch with Stephen, and Stephen said SWAT had arrived but that everyone was trying to avoid any shooting. Then, Blanch put Stephen on with Mr. Meade for a few minutes. After the call, Mr. Meade got in touch with the Good Morning America reporter and let her know what was happening. Beatrice reached out to all the local news stations for the same reason, and everyone agreed to stay away. They'd report on the events, but from down the road. No one wanted to give into this homegrown terrorist's demands.

None of us could quite figure out how Johnny Tucker knew we were going to talk to the national news, but it seemed obvious he knew because why else would he make himself the focus of the story. He seemed to think he could, as Isaiah said, "Control the narrative." But Johnny Tucker kept underestimating us, underestimating everyone, really.

We stayed hunkered down below the windows for a while, and it seemed like things were at a standstill. This was the moment.

I took a deep breath and said, "I need to go out there."

Every face in the room looked at me, but Blanch was the first to move. "I don't think that's a good idea."

The chorus of "me neither" was quite loud, and I appreciated their concern. But I knew what I needed to do.

"I need to go out there. I just do. Javier, Blanch, you can come with me. Beatrice, can you get a camera crew up here to the school safely?"

Beatrice looked at my mom, who nodded slowly and then said to me, "I can. But Mary, are you sure?"

"Yes. I'm sure."

Mrs. Garrison gave me a hug and a knowing smile. Then, Blanch called the office, and they unlocked the classroom door just long enough for the three of us to slip out and down the hall.

I know it probably seemed like my friends and especially my mom should have pushed harder to get me to stay, made me stay in that room even. But they knew it would do no good. They would have had to hold me down to get me not to walk out of that room, and no one wanted to do that. Even if they were scared of what would happen to me, we'd all learned that sometimes the scariest option is the best one.

Two minutes later, I was standing on the lawn of the high school by the flag, face to face with Johnny Tucker. Overhead, I could hear a drone; Beatrice's colleague was flying it, and I knew everyone had their phones to the glass windows in the rooms around the courtyard. Javier also had his camera on so that the news station had footage with sound. It was quite the impromptu production.

"Mary Steele, thank you for meeting with me."

"It wasn't as if you gave me much choice, Mr. Tucker. You're holding my friends hostage."

"Now, let's not go using nasty words like *hostage*. They are just a bit of insurance is all."

"I'm not going to play games, Mr. Tucker. What you are doing here is terrorism. You don't like something, and so to get your way, you're trying to scare me and everyone else into being quiet. You're just like Timothy McVeigh and the men who flew the planes into buildings on September eleventh."

"Listen here, missy"—I almost laughed out loud because he sounded so much like a caricature of an angry old man—"I am nothing like those Muslims. They were evil. I'm just trying to protect the heritage of our town."

"No, sir. You're trying to protect the false image of your heritage. You're trying to protect a heritage built on your whiteness, on the privilege that being white has given you and that has allowed your family to hurt black people in Terra Linda. You aren't trying to protect us"—I pointed up at all the faces in the windows around us—"and honestly, you just think you're protecting yourself."

I could see his face getting red, and I knew he wanted to say something, but I didn't give him a chance. "The sad thing is, though, that you aren't really even protecting yourself. You're just entrenching yourself in hatred, which harms both the people you hate and you. Racism doesn't just hurt people of color. It hurts us white people too. It leaves us trapped in shame and guilt, and it separates us from people who could love us, teach us, treasure us, and give us the honor of doing the same to them."

I took a deep breath and felt Javier's hand between my

shoulder blades, a gentle comfort. "Besides, everyone already knows about the cemetery, and now, they're going to know that the people buried there were all killed by your father or his predecessors. That's right, I know your father led the lynch mob that killed a lot of those people, and I expect that he was just following in his father's, your grandfather's, footsteps. It was the family legacy. Is that the heritage you want to protect?"

All the color had drained from Johnny Tucker's face. He kept opening and closing his mouth like he wanted to say something but kept finding that the words had slipped back down his throat.

"But you see, Mr. Tucker, I'm not here to try to humiliate you or to silence you. I'm not here to try to get you to feel guilty about something you didn't do, because guilt makes us do ugly things when we can't make right the things that were done wrong. When we feel guilty or ashamed, when we hide what happened instead of confessing what we've done wrong and bringing it into the light so we can see what – if any – responsibility we have for the thing we are carrying, that ugliness begins to grow in us. It becomes a massive twist of ugly right in the middle of ourselves, and over time, all we can do is try to hide it, even as it gets bigger and bigger and takes over more and more of ourselves."

I didn't know where these words were coming from, but they were true, and I could feel the power riding them. "I don't want to shame you, Mr. Tucker. I don't want to lash you or make you feel guilty. I just want to offer you a chance to admit to what your family did, not because you can do anything about it and not because admitting it makes it all right, but because by letting a little light in on that dark, twisted thing, you can begin to let it go, begin to heal, begin to open up again."

I extended my hand to the old man in front of me. Before, I had only been able to see his twisted ugliness, but now, I saw the truth of who he was, who he had been since that awful day ninety years ago: a little boy who had watched his dad kill two people because he didn't like that his son loved them. Johnny Tucker was still that little boy who stole that knife. He'd let that moment at the lock seize him up and shut him down because it was the only way he could live with the awfulness that his father had done. He had to latch on to the ugly or else he had to risk losing the love he had for his father. I shuddered at the thought of what it would mean if my mother had done something so terrible, of how hard it would be to figure out how to love her even though.

Johnny Tucker looked at my hand; he looked at Javier standing just behind me; he looked up at all the windows around us. Then, he looked at my hand again, turned, and walked away.

I hadn't expected different. I had hoped, but I hadn't expected. Giving up hate is scary. It leaves a big open space in a person, and empty is a hard thing to feel, even when it's the only way to have the chance at love.

Within minutes, all of Johnny's people had followed him out of the school driveway. The police had arrested the four men in the classroom, and all the buses were rolling up to take everyone home. And I still had time to get to the lock for my interview.

---

18

*T*he interview was fine. After all the events of the day, I ended up not being nervous. Something about confronting a terrorist on national TV (it ended up being breaking national news) puts even the most intimidating of interviews in perspective. The reporter was kind, and when I didn't want to be specific about things—say exactly how I'd found the cemetery and when—she didn't push. She treated me as someone giving her a gift rather than someone trying to hide something, and I so appreciated that.

While I talked, my friends stayed nearby but out of camera view. They're moral supporters to the end. I was facing away from the river so that the camerawoman could film the hill where the cemetery stood, and I knew, somehow, that Bo and Sarah were up there watching. And when I finished, I turned and gave them the tiniest of waves. Their smiles matched mine.

After the news team packed up and headed off, Mom ran to Dunkin' and got a steaming-hot box of cocoa for all of us. Everyone milled around texting folks and making live videos to tell everyone that we'd be on Good Morning America the next morning.

Mrs. Garrison and I sat at our picnic table in the warm spring sun. The reporter had interviewed her, too, and she'd told her family story, including the bits about who her grandfather was and how her mother had died. She didn't share that Johnny Tucker had taken the knife that her mother had brought to the lynching scene. As she told me later, she didn't figure people would be kind to him about that fact, and she didn't think more cruelty would help him be less cruel.

I was grateful for Mrs. Garrison's kindness, to Mr. Tucker and to me, and I hoped she'd have a bit more to give. I needed to talk to someone who understood the whole ghost thing.

Mrs. Garrison leaned back against the table behind her and stretched her legs out toward the river. "So you okay?"

I stretched out my legs, too, and thought about her question. The day before, my answer would have been definitely not, but today, something had shifted. I'd settled into myself, accepted something about what my gift meant, found some courage maybe. "Yeah, I think so. I mean, I don't know that I'll ever love this," I spun my hand around in circles, "whatever *this* is, but I'm okay."

"Good. Sometimes, the best way of being is just okay. We can't change everything. Some things we just have to accept."

I nodded and turned to face her on the bench. "I need to ask you something." I needed to know what else Mrs. Garrison could do that I could, so I told her about my teleportation—because I guess that's what it was.

She shook her head. "Nope, honey. I can't do that." She put her hand on mine. "You got a full measure more of weird than I did."

I smiled. Weird was right. I told her about how the first times it happened, I had been caught completely off guard, but now, I was beginning to feel it, to know it was coming, and that I thought maybe I could even will it when I wanted.

"I expect you'll learn more and more. Now, after all these years, I know when I'm about to see a ghost. I can feel them before I even see them. Some sort of tingle or something, a little tug toward a place."

"Yes, that's it. That's what I feel when I'm about to travel."

Mrs. Garrison nodded. "This is a lot, Mary, this thing we do. It's heavy. But when we know it's coming, it means we can also walk away. I expect that you—like me—will never make that choice, but there's a gift in having the option, in the freedom to choose not to."

There was that word again, *freedom*. We throw it around with all our patriotism and slogans. We talk about it like it's a battle cry. But the more I learned about and the more I reached into the history of racism, the more I saw it as an honor, something bestowed to all of us and more often taken away from some than won back by others.

I knew what she meant. This peacefulness, this acceptance, it came because now I could choose this gift, or not choose it. The choice didn't change a thing about the gift itself or how I might live into it, but it sure did change how I felt.

I thought of Moses and his family: of the way their lives were entirely circumscribed by slavery, of how they had no choices about anything. I thought about Charlotte and those kids, how that fiction of the man Jim Crow had killed them, even as he ripped their justice away too.

Sometimes people want to talk about the slave days or about Jim Crow as being "better than *x*," comparing how bad some people had it as a justification for why it wasn't so bad for other people. But the material circumstances of a life—the access to food and water, clean clothes, education—those were important things, crucial things, necessary rights. But the opportunity to choose, the chance to intervene in the way your life, your day, your next minute would go . . . when that is denied a person, the spirit gets burdened, and can, without the greatest of strength, simply break.

On the hill across the river, I could see Sarah and her mother. They were watching us, serene and staid. I knew I needed to go over there, could feel the tug on my sternum, but I also knew I had time, that the pull would stay until I answered it or decided not to.

"When do your ghosts move on, Mrs. Garrison?"

"Girl, don't you think it's about time you called me Josephine?"

I grinned. "Yes, ma'am. Do you do something special to help them leave, um, Josephine?"

She stared up at her mother and grandmother, her face still but pensive. "Best I can figure, I help them tell someone something they needed to hear."

"Like the Ghost Whisperer?" I regretted it as soon as I said it. A ninety-four-year-old woman did not watch ghost dramas.

"Yes, ma'am. Melinda Gordon and I are so much alike." I must have looked surprised because she laughed and said, "You think I don't watch all those ghost shows too? I have the full set on DVD."

I laughed hard then. Just the image of Mrs. Garrison watching Jennifer Love Hewitt help people into the light was enough to make me cry with laughter.

"But yes, like that. My work seems to be a private one, about carrying words forward, about retying threads of families and friends." She turned toward me then and looked me in the eye. "But you, Mary, your work is a public one, I think. You need to bring things into the light, not walk people toward it."

I knew she was right. Even now, I could feel that Sarah and Bo would be moving on soon, that they were just waiting a bit for me, and I knew they were ready because we'd found the cemetery and told the story of the people buried there.

In fact, Shamila had just told me the historical society was going to have a full issue dedicated to the stories of the people in those unmarked graves. It would tell the story of their lives and their deaths—I'd written down all the names that Bo had told me and passed them on to Shamila.

Plus, I'd heard Isaiah and Mom talking about another memorial service for everyone buried there and a marker, too, but one that would be placed here, next to Bo's at the site of her death, because they didn't want to risk people desecrating the cemetery by identifying just where it was. I knew, though, that they'd let the Department of Historic Resources know about it so it could be verified and mapped and, thus, protected from development and destruction.

So my work, it was done. But I still had a question.

"But why me, Mrs. Gar—, I mean Josephine? Why do I have to do this work publicly?"

Mrs. Garrison took a deep breath as she gazed over the Maury. Then, she turned to me again. "Because you're white, Mary. You have black roots, yes, and that's important, so important. But this work, this is a work of repair, of reparation. It's a work that needs to be done by someone who carries the privilege that comes with living in white skin. It's a bigger, wider burden because white people carry the responsibility of this history of violence and racism."

She reached over and took my hand. "I expect that doesn't feel fair, like you're being asked to carry the burden of a whole lot more than you owe."

I knew what she meant, and yes, it was a big weight. But I didn't resent it. More, I wanted to share it, wanted more white people to carry it with me because I couldn't do this alone, because this was our work, damage we had done—were still doing—and damage that only we could make reparations for.

Then, though, I looked over and saw my friends, all their skin tones, all their histories. I saw my mom and Isaiah, who I expected would be my step-father soon. I saw Marcie and Nicole and hoped their relationship would last. I saw Javier and felt my heart lift. Beatrice, Shamila, Mr. Meade, Blanch, Stephen—all these people who had helped me carry this burden so far, . . . and I knew the burden was being carried by many, not enough yet, but by many.

I squeezed Josephine's hand.

So much of history was about people doing more than their fair share. More than their fair share of hate and harm, but also more than their fair share of healing. It would be easy to become resentful, to try to cast off burdens that felt too much. But as I sat there holding hands with a ninety-four-year-old black woman whose grandmother and mother had been killed because they loved a white man, whose uncle had threatened to kill high school students to hide his shame, who had lived her whole life seeing ghosts of people she had a responsibility to bring to peace, I knew my burden was light.

Nat Turner, Claudette Colvin, Malcolm X, Dr. King, Ella Baker—those people had been the faces for moments that were much larger than their own names. They had carried the burden of being known, but they weren't alone. And I wasn't either.

"I'll be okay. It'll be okay."

Josephine smiled at me. "Okay is good. It is enough."

She stood and hugged me, and then she walked over to her giant car, waving to everyone as she went, her white cane slung up and over her shoulder. I smiled.

But then, it was time for another, longer goodbye. I waved to Mom and raised my pointer finger in what had become, already, the sign we would use for the rest of her life. And I went up to Bo and Sarah.

Our goodbye was short, a few words of gratitude exchanged from one to the other, rightful in their sharing. I told them I was so grateful to know them, to have learned their story—both the ugly parts and the gorgeous ones. I thanked them for letting me be the one to bring in a little light. They smiled.

"You are light, Mary," Sarah said. "You shine bright. Don't forget that. You be. That's all we need. Just you be."

Tears streamed down my face, and Bo reached over and wiped my cheek. "Child, you strong. Don't you forget that. But don't let nobody tell you that weak is wrong. We all weak sometimes." She hugged me. "The thing is you just keep going even in the weak. That way, you find the strong again."

They were starting to fade, starting to slide back or up or out to where they belonged. Sarah reached over and hugged me tight, a bone-crushing hug like her daughter always gave, and I kissed her cheek as she slid away.

When I traveled back to my living friends, I felt something give way within me, like I'd removed a splinter I didn't know I'd had, . . . and I knew then that my time traveling here at the lock was over. It felt like a relief and a promise all at once.

The next day, Mom and I moved back home. Stephen had said it was safe to go back because he didn't believe Johnny Tucker would try anything again. I invited everyone over so I could explain that it seemed I had a bit of control over how I "moved" when it came to the ghosts I saw.

"So you can choose when you see them?" Marcie asked.

"No, not like that. It's more like I know when I'll go but not where or who will be there when I show up. More like I can move once the story begins but not until someone else decides I need to be a part of the story."

I don't think they got it, but they didn't care. They could see something had changed in me, I guess, that I was more reconciled. So they didn't ask more questions.

"Whenever for whatever, Mary, you know we've got your back," Javier said as he winked at me.

I blushed, but when I looked around the room at all my friends there, people I had known my entire life and people who I had only met because of this journey, I felt no embarrassment at all. These folks had stepped up beside me even when the weirdest things in the world happened, even when we were in danger for our lives, even when we had to find our way through the messy pain of history and now. These were my people, and they always would be. I knew that for sure.

EPILOGUE

I've been traveling now for twenty-eight years. Most of the time, I feel the pull before it takes me, but even now, it sometimes catches me unaware and I find myself shoeless in some place around my hometown. I've never moved—never wanted to and never felt like it was the right thing to do.

OVER THE YEARS, I've seen dozens of ghosts—every single one of them black, every single one of them killed because of that fact. Each time, my friends—the ones who stayed in Terra Linda like Mom and Isaiah, Shamila, Mr. Meade, and Blanch, and the ones who moved away like Marcie and Nicole, Javier, and Beatrice—rallied with research and wisdom, moral support and publicity. Our relationships changed—Javier and I didn't make it long-term, but we stayed friends, and I married that awkward red-head Blanch who has acted as my own personal bodyguard for going on twenty years now—but the fact that we worked together on these horrors that I saw never shifted at all. These friendships have been the greatest relationships of my life.

· · ·

I ENDED UP BEING A WRITER. It seemed like writing about and sharing all the horror and beauty I saw was another way I could make sense everything. Sometimes, I wrote nonfiction: essays or magazine articles about the facts of what had happened. And sometimes, the stories became fictional in name and place but not in truth or reality. I never wrote about something I didn't have permission to tell from the living as well as, when possible, from the dead. To tell someone else's story is a great responsibility. The opportunity to do that important work is a gift, and when it's not given freely, it's theft. White people have stolen enough people's stories already. I never want to do that. Ever.

TONIGHT, in the living room of the farmhouse by the stream, just up from the cemetery that began all these blessed, brutal adventures, I am nostalgic for the days when I was young and this journey was new. Then, I didn't take anything for granted because I knew nothing. Now, I'm a bit more jaded, a bit less hopeful of happy endings and the possibility of healing. A quarter century of watching people's ugliness go wild can tarnish a person's hope.

NONE of the stories I've been honored to witness and help bring into the light has ended with a storybook resolution. As much as I wish we could just all hug it out sometimes, that never happens. Instead, some small change comes. I'm reminded of that old Leonard Cohen song: "There is a crack, a crack in everything. That's how the light gets in." I'm just trying to make a few cracks.

SO I KEEP TRYING, even when I'm tired. I remember Josephine. I think of the note she left for me when she died: "Carry on, Mary. Remember that you must only do what you can do, nothing more, but nothing less, either." Then, I muster up the light in my spirit as much as I can when I feel the tug to travel. Every time I see that new face of the person who died violently, I try to remember that this might be the time when people will finally own the shadows that live inside us all and let the light shine through.

THEN, I do what I can do. I shine my light. I tell the story. I hug the people close to me and let them help me too. I tell the truth, and I let it be.

AT NIGHT, when I tuck my son in, when I look at his gentle face, I lean close and say, "I love you. Rest well. I'll see you when the light comes back."

AUTHOR'S NOTE

Obviously, this is a work of fiction. . . . Or at least, it is in my world. I've never seen or talked to a ghost, and to be honest, I'm not sure what I really think about their existence . . . although I do watch all the ghost shows like Mary and Josephine.

But the historical events that prompted these stories, they are as real and historical as it gets. The specific events in these three books are fictional creations of mine, but they are based on real-life stories and experiences that I've studied in my work as a historian. Moses's, Charlotte's, and Sarah and Bo's stories could very easily have happened, and sadly, similarly terrible events did occur.

My hope is that Mary's experiences spark conversations, encourage learning and study, prompt reckoning, and, in some small way, bring healing. That's a lofty job for any piece of writing, but it remains my prayer nonetheless.

I am deeply indebted to many, many black people who have graciously taught me—yet another white woman—what their lived experience has been and who have gifted me with their stories and the stories of their families. My prayer is that these works make them proud and that they will forgive the missteps I have surely made.

I am also profoundly grateful to the members of two organizations, The Central Virginia History Researchers (CVHR) in Charlottesville, Virginia and Coming to the Table. The members of CVHR have helped me begin to understand the black history of our city, a history that became national news in 2017 when white supremacists took to our streets. CVHR is the organization that has grounded me in history and the important—often silenced—history of black communities, and I am forever grateful for their support and their deeply valuable, unpaid work to preserve, record, and share the black history of Central Virginia.

Coming to the Table, oh, what can I say about the group of people who have challenged me, as a white woman, more than any other? The members of this organization have forced me to reckon with my own racism, taught me how to be deeply proud of my black ancestors, encouraged me to take risks in talking and writing about racial and racist history, and forgiven me when I have screwed up royally in these endeavors. Coming to the Table has, at its core, the central knowledge that racism harms all of us, no matter our ethnicity, because it separates us, shames us, and wounds us. Without the members of Coming to the Table, I would be far less rich in my friendships and far, far more wounded in my spirit.

I believe firmly that it is our responsibility as white people to make amends—and yes, pay reparations—for the harm we have done to African Americans in our nation. The ways we do that are myriad and personal. They are institutional and individual. But they all begin with an inward journey to see what shadows we harbor and what racism lives within us because if we are white, we have been taught to be racist, whether we realize it or not, whether that teaching was overt or not. The United States is a nation that privileges whiteness and always has, and until we are willing to look into ourselves and shine light on the shadows within ourselves, we cannot begin to break down the white supremacist systems that continue to—on a daily basis—oppress the people of color in our midst.

Our nation was built on the backs of Native American and African people. To oppress people in such a profound way, an entire people—in this case, white people—was taught, for generations, that such oppression is right. It is hard work to undo that teaching, but it is not impossible work.

We can do this. We can heal ourselves and our nation. I believe that even on my weariest days, even when I cannot understand how my sisters and brothers of color carry on in the work. I believe it always because to not believe is to give up hope, . . . and that I cannot do.

We need you—whether you see ghosts or not, whether you live in the South or not, whether you drive past fields or ride the subway under skyscrapers, whether you are ninety-four, like Josephine, or sixteen, like Mary. We need your light. We need your voice. We need your journey, no matter where you may start from.

The key is not how far down the road you are but that you are on the road at all. Read history as it is written by the people who lived it amongst the shadows. Read history written by people of color and indigenous people. Research the acts of racism in your own community. Share those stories with the people you know. Write a letter to the editor of your local paper. Shine the light. Even a tiny beam is a way forward in a tunnel of darkness.

If you would like to begin or continue your journey in this work of healing, I highly recommend that you explore Coming to the Table—www.comingtothetable.org. We have local groups all over the country, and we have a robust national group on social media with bi-annual gatherings in person. We welcome you to the table. We will sit with you there while you find your footing amongst your own shadows (and our own), and we will help you shine the light.

To learn more about the Equal Justice Initiative's National Memorial for Justice and Peace, visit their website—https://eji.org/national-lynching-memorial.

Enjoy ALL the books in the *Steele Secrets* series.

Available everywhere books are sold.

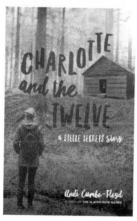

Ghosts. Spells. People with Wild Abilities.

If these are your faves, then come on over and get all the
magical realism books your TBR can handle. Weekly
emails of magical realism and fantasy, especially for
young adults and the young at heart. Plus, a few notices
about my own books, too.

Join my newsletter here – Andilit.com/magicalrealism.

ABOUT THE AUTHOR

Andi Cumbo-Floyd is a writer, editor, and writing coach who lives at the edge of the Blue Ridge Mountains with her husband, 4 dogs, 4 cats, 6 goats, and 28 chickens. Her previous books include *The Slaves Have Names* and *Love Letters to Writers*. You can find out more about her books at andilit.com.

.

facebook.com/andilitwriter

twitter.com/andilit

instagram.com/andicumbofloyd

Made in the USA
Middletown, DE
02 April 2019